FOCUS ON THE FAMILY® PRESENTS

adventures of AVERAGE BOY™

GROWING UP SUPER AVERAGE

by comedian **Bob Smiley** and **Jesse Florea**

TYNDALE

Tyndale House Publishers, Inc.
Carol Stream, Illinois

A Focus on the Family book published by
Tyndale House Publishers, Inc., Carol Stream, Illinois 60188
Focus on the Family and the accompanying logo and design are federally registered trademarks of Focus on the Family, Colorado Springs, CO 80995.

TYNDALE and Tyndale's quill logo are registered trademarks of Tyndale House Publishers, Inc.

Average Boy is a registered trademark of Focus on the Family.

Some characters are the product of the author's imagination, while others are loosely based on real people (like his parents). Names and the details of events have been changed to protect the identity of those individuals—and Bob Smiley.

Editor: Kathy Davis
Illustrations by Gary Locke
Cover design by Jon Collins
Interior design by Jeff Lane/Brandango.us

Library of Congress Cataloging-in-Publication Data

Smiley, Bob.
Growing up super average : the adventures of average boy / Bob Smiley &
Jesse Florea. -- 1st ed.
p. cm.
"A Focus on the Family book."
ISBN-13: 978-1-58997-441-8
ISBN-10: 1-58997-441-7
1. Boys--Religious life. 2. Teenage boys--Religious life. I. Florea,
Jesse, 1970- II. Title.
BV4541.3.S65 2007
248.8'2--dc22
2007009835

Printed in the United States of America
  2 3 4 5 6 7 8 9 / 13 12 11 10 09 08

I dedicate this book to all my schoolteachers who loved me enough to put my desk right next to theirs. Also, a special thanks to Trent, Zander, Colter, Mom and Dad, and the beautiful Wendy! If it weren't for you, there would be different names listed here in this dedication . . . oh, and I wouldn't have all these stories, either! I love you all.

—*Bob*

For Nate, Amber, and every kid who's on the awesome adventure of following God. Strive to be super average!

—*Jesse*

TABLE OF CONTENTS

Meet Average Boy

Name: Bob Smiley

Middle Name: something worse than "Gertrude"

Height: five feet four inches, up to five feet five in a strong wind

Weight: 94 pounds without cape (98 pounds with cape; 100 pounds with cape soaking wet!)

Favorite Sport: Kickball

Best Friend: Billy (You'll see why after reading this book.)

Favorite Food: Chocolat . . . uh . . . my mom says it's broccoli

Greatest Quantity of Food Eaten at One Time: Six hot dogs at Billy's birthday party. (Note: Two of them stayed with me!)

Favorite Book: Used to be *How to Get Out of Trouble* by Billy (only one copy in circulation). Now it's a new book: *Growing Up Super Average*

Favorite Color: Depends what wall I'm painting

Favorite Subject in School: English, becauze I'm am really very well at it

Daily Chores: Cleaning room, cleaning paint off walls, feeding my pets, mowing the lawn, apologizing to my brother

Greatest Accomplishment: Telling people about Jesus

Favorite Bible Verse: Joshua 1:9

Favorite Hero from Bible: Jesus (Anyone who will die for me is the kind of hero I want!)

Favorite Adult: Tie between my parents, because they're always there for me

Favorite Hobby: Playing outside

Least Favorite Hobby: Filling out these answers

THE QUEST TO BECOME SUPER AVERAGE

1

Being a popular superhero is awesome! Fans always notice me and stop me in public. Once I got noticed by eight different people in one hour! Of course, my dad likes to point out that we were at a family reunion. But I know my dad was just jealous of my fame.

"They didn't seem to notice you, Dad," I said.

"Anyone would get noticed if he wears a cape," my dad argued.

Before we went to the reunion, I suggested Dad could wear my bedspread for a cape. But he wasn't interested. I guess some people just don't want to be

Growing Up Super Average

super. Others, including me, want to be super, but it doesn't come naturally.

I wasn't always Average Boy. When I started middle school, I knew I had to find my place, my crowd, my peeps. This proved to be difficult, especially because I wasn't really sure what a "peep" was at the time. I knew I wasn't supposed to utter one during detention and I liked eating them at Easter, but that's all I had figured out.

On the first day of school, I looked around to see where I'd fit in. I started with the jocks. These kids looked like a doctor had removed their necks and reattached the skin and muscle to their biceps and chests. They were so big that when they turned around, their shadows sent an eclipse moving over the room. I'm not totally sure, but I think each shadow weighed about 12 pounds. All the jocks had armpit hair and could palm a basketball—with me still holding on to it.

I figured with a few changes, I could fit in with these giants—I mean, kids. First, I stuck two strips of duct tape on my cat. Pulling them off wasn't as easy. But to be a jock, you have to be good at wrestling. Once I had ripped off the duct tape and superglued it under my armpits, I started working on palming a basketball.

That didn't go so well either. I discovered I

could palm a Wiffle ball—just not for very long! But I still thought I could pull off being a jock. After all, I had armpit hair and my shadow had gained a pound or two since I started eating protein bars to build muscle.

During the first day of gym, I walked over and stood next to Colter, the best athlete in school.

"What are you doing over here, little boy?" Colter asked. "We don't need a water bottle yet."

Did You Know?

- Studies show that popular kids are more likely to drink alcohol, smoke, shoplift, and vandalize property than average kids.
- A recent survey found that 37 percent of popular kids grew up to be less successful in life than unpopular kids.
- It's impossible to tell the popular kids apart because they all dress the same and are named either Ashley or Nick.

Warning: One out of three statistics may contain false information and defame the name of all the nice Ashleys and Nicks.

The rest of the jocks laughed.

"Oh, I heard you did," I replied. "But now that I've talked to you, I realize you need a bottle of mouthwash."

Sometimes my mouth doesn't like me and tries to get me in trouble. The jocks took it really well, though. They even asked me to play catch with them—I just wish they hadn't used me as the ball.

This got me to thinking that maybe the "brains" were more my crowd. During study hall, I went over to their table. They were playing chess. It was Trent's turn, the smartest kid in school.

"My rook takes your knight," Trent said as his opponent looked defeated. "That means Trent-Baggins has reclaimed his ring and can disappear from this game. Checkmate!"

"Wow, your castle took his horsey!" I yelled, trying to fit in.

Quickly, all the brains looked up through their glasses. One of them pointed at me and said something in what I think was Klingon. Everyone laughed.

I decided I might join the band. The problem with band is that you have to play an instrument. I decided I'd learn how to play the piano. Then I found out it was a marching band. I figured I might slow up everybody if I had to scoot around on a piano stool, so I took up the triangle.

We all got cool nicknames in the band. I was Bob "No Rhythm" Smiley. I earned a spot as fifth triangle alternate. This confused me because there weren't four other alternates—much less a *regular* triangle player. After not being allowed on the field for two games, I left the band. I didn't mind really. I couldn't wear that band hat without laughing.

That left just the skater crowd. However, I knew I didn't want to hang with them. They did stuff I didn't agree with, like grind rails without head protection. I knew God didn't want me making the wrong kind of friends. Plus, they were mean to me when I tried talking to them. One of the skater kids even spit on me. I have to say, though, it was a pretty impressive feat because I was about 30 feet away and against the wind. She was good.

To be honest, I was kind of discouraged. Three weeks into school and no peeps. I had tried my hardest—I had the armpit rash to prove it. I just wasn't supertalented at any one thing.

That's when it hit me: I was just average. In fact, I was all-around super average! The Bible talks about lots of people who were just average, and yet God used them for great things. I knew right then that God had called me to be Average Boy!

On the spot, I decided to fight injustice and do

my best using the average talents my Creator had given me! Even though I'm average, my God isn't. So I know I'm already going to win in the end. Isn't that cool?!? You can be on the winning team, too, if you're part of my team—I mean God's team. Anyway, that's what this book is about. I hope you enjoy reading these adventures, my peeps!

Super Average Advice

Some kids are born with a ton of athletic talent. Others can pick up an instrument and immediately play a beautiful melody. Speaking of beauty, some kids have got it. As you look around, you'll see kids who automatically fit in.

Maybe navigating your way through life isn't always that easy. You don't click with the popular crowd. When you pick up an instrument and play, you draw a crowd—but it's a pack of howling dogs. The truth is, growing up can be difficult. You may make mistakes. But there are some things you can do to make the most of life's adventure.

Be a friend. If you want to find where you fit in, you have to be friendly. Try different things. Reach out to other kids. Be a friend to someone who's lonely. Don't try to become something you're not, just so you can fit in with the popular crowd. Proverbs 18:24 says, "A man of many companions may come to ruin, but there is a friend who sticks closer than a brother." Having a lot of friends isn't always the best thing. You can be pulled in different directions and forget who God created you to be. Try to be a true, loyal friend. You already have the best friend you could have in Jesus.

Give your life to God. You may feel average, but God doesn't look at you that way. He has an amazing plan for your life. All you have to do is follow God's guidebook—the Bible—and trust Him. God specializes in making the ordinary extraordinary. Check out these words written by the apostle Paul: "Take your everyday, ordinary life . . . and place it before God as an offering. Embracing what God does for you is the best thing you can do for him" (Romans 12:1, MSG). If you feel average, that's great! Give what you are to God. Offer your life to Him and then stand back and watch the miracles He can do.

God's Guide

Read: 2 Corinthians 12:9-10
- When is God's power made perfect?
- How does God want you to feel when you hit difficult times and someone makes fun of your faith?
- Write down what you think this means: "When I am weak, then I am strong."

_____

_____

_____

Bonus Activity

Want to be a superhero, too? Just follow the guidelines above and ask your mom to make you a mask and cape.

TRUE FRIENDSHIP

2

Billy (my best friend) and I love cereal, especially Cocoa Puffs. One morning after Billy and I camped out in my backyard, I discovered that a Cocoa Puff fit perfectly into my nostril. I stuffed one in and said, "Hey, Billy, do I have something in my nose?"

Billy exploded with laughter. "Yeah, I think it's a dung beetle. Did it rent an apartment in your nose?"

I quickly grabbed another Cocoa Puff and put it in my other nostril.

"Wow, something smells chocolately!" I said, laughing.

A minute later, I had two Cocoa Puffs in each nostril. That's when I started having trouble breathing through my nose. But I couldn't stop laughing.

I pulled out two of the Cocoa Puffs. Then I realized I couldn't reach the first two that were now mashed pretty far up into my nose.

"They're stuck!" I said, no longer laughing.

Billy suggested I shove an eviction notice up my nose to kick out the other two apartment renters. He obviously still found humor in the situation. I, on the other hand, was starting to panic.

I didn't want to go to my parents, because we'd already been to the hospital once to get a small rubber ball out of my nose. My dad had even made me write a hundred times that I wouldn't put a rubber ball in my nose ever again. In my defense, I haven't put one anywhere near my nose since. But I doubt my dad would see the difference between a rubber ball and a Cocoa Puff—even though scientifically I could probably prove they have different molecular structures.

"Billy, I'm serious," I said. "We have to get these out."

Billy jumped into action, grabbing my nose with his hand and squeezing really hard.

KRRRUUUUNNNNNNNCHHHHHHHHH!

I felt the Cocoa Puffs break into tiny pieces. (It

was either that or the cartilage in my nose.) It hurt like crazy. In fact, I started crying and **chocolate milk** began pouring out of my nose. That fixed the Cocoa Puffs problem.

It's awesome to have a true friend like Billy. A true friend knows when you're serious and when you're joking. A true friend will jump in and help you out—even if it's going to hurt. And a true friend won't laugh at you when you cry. Billy is a true friend.

We've been friends for years. I met Billy out on the dirt road in front of our house. He was riding his bike . . . kind of. Actually, he was attempting to stand with one foot on his bike seat and one foot on his handlebars. I was so amazed that I shouted, "Wow!" Looking back, I should've said it a little more quietly, because I evidently frightened my cat, which I was holding. The cat jumped out of my arms and ran into the road. Billy saw the cat flying toward him and tried to swerve. He missed my cat . . . and hit a ditch.

"That was awesome!" I said running over to him. "I'm Bob. What's your name?"

"People call me Crazy Billy, although I don't know why," he said as he lay in the ditch covered with mud and broken bike parts.

We became best friends right away and started

hanging out at each other's houses. Actually, we hung out outside of our houses, because our parents thought we needed some space to play. We chased cows. We swam in the creek. We ran from cows. I took Billy to church. We rode bikes. We fixed our bikes. And we started a Band-Aid collection on our bodies. It was great!

The next week Billy and I tried playing Frisbee in my driveway. But the Frisbee was superlight and couldn't go into the wind. I thought it would fly better if we taped a big rock to it. This actually worked well . . . too well. One time when Billy threw the Frisbee to me, it sailed over my head and crashed into my dad's windshield. It cracked into a

Did You Know?

- A recent survey found that Americans have fewer close friends than they did 20 years ago.
- Fun words for *friend* include: *companion, chum, confidant, buddy, compatriot, pal, cohort,* and *sidekick*.
- The computer is not your friend, even if it beeps lovingly when you hit the keys and tells you when you have mail.

million pieces—the windshield, not the rock.

Moments later my dad came running outside.

"Bob! What did you do?" he shouted.

"I . . . uh," I started to say.

"Mr. Smiley, I did it," Billy jumped in. "I threw the Frisbee. It was my fault. I'll pay for it or work it off."

I couldn't believe it. A lot of kids would've stayed quiet or run away. But Billy is a true friend. He knows true friends stand up for each other. Since then, we've had many chances to stand up for one another. You just can't beat having a good friend!

A lot of kids pick friends based on popularity. However, popularity doesn't help when you're in a jam. I hope you'll find a few true friends in your life and stay away from kids who encourage you not to be yourself.

Now if you'll excuse me, I have to go tell my dad why his glass of chocolate milk tastes funny.

Super Average Advice

Few things feel better than having a true friend in your life—except maybe a cold glass of lemonade on a steamy summer day. No, a true friend *is* better, because a real friend will never leave a sour taste in your mouth.

Finish this sentence:

When I tell a joke that I think is funny, my friend . . .

   a) laughs.
   b) groans.
   c) asks, "Who are you?"
   d) says, "I don't get it."

If you answered *a,* you know how great it feels to have a true friend. If you answered *d,* you may need to find a friend who isn't blonde (just kidding). And if you didn't answer *a,* you should look for the following characteristics for future friends.

They allow you to be yourself. You don't have to change your personality or preferences to fit in with real friends. True friends don't make fun of you because you like wearing socks with your flip-flops or enjoy collecting all your toenail clippings. (Note: I'm up to two shoeboxes full!) Around a real friend, you can always be the unique and fun person God created you to be. You may not always get your way or do exactly what you want to do, but you'll always feel accepted.

They help you be your best. True friends won't encourage you to do something that you know you shouldn't, such as ditching your responsibilities at home or disobeying your parents. Instead they'll point you in the right direction—

toward God. First Thessalonians 5:11 says, "Encourage one another and build each other up." True friends will support you when you try something new . . . and may even try it with you.

They're not afraid to tell you that you're wrong. Having a true friend isn't all fun and games. Sometimes deep friendships can hurt. But you can tell you have a true friend if he or she cares enough about you to tell you when you're messing up. The Bible puts it this way: "Faithful are the wounds of a friend, but the kisses of an enemy are deceitful" (Proverbs 27:6, NKJV).

A person who's not your friend may treat you nicely just to get something from you. Once your usefulness is gone, you'll get dropped like a greased pig. But a friend will tell you the truth, even if the truth hurts. Parents and pastors love to talk about *accountability*, which is a fancy way to say, "You watch out for your friend and he'll watch out for you." Do your best to find an accountability buddy now, and you'll have a smoother road in the future. And if you see a friend making a mistake by doing things like experimenting with alcohol or looking at inappropriate Web sites, be a real friend and point out the dangers.

GOD'S GUIDE

Read: John 15:12-15

- What does Jesus say is the ultimate way to show love for friends? What did Jesus do for you?
- What does Jesus want you to do to show that you're His friend?
- Why do you think Jesus now calls you a friend? How does that make you feel?

_____

_____

_____

BONUS ACTIVITY

Put on an old swimsuit, and grab a liter of Diet Coke and two Mentos mints. Set the Diet Coke on the ground where it won't mess up anything. Drop the two Mentos mints into the bottle and wait for the fireworks. Diet Coke will spew out of the bottle about three feet into the air. You and a friend can stand on either side of the "fountain" and see who gets the most soda in his or her mouth. The winner can eat what's left of the Mentos.

3

I was standing by my locker thinking up excuses for why I hadn't done my math homework when Donny walked up and pushed me.

Donny *is* his name, but my friends and I sometimes call him "Huh?" because he says it all the time. Of course, we don't call him that to his face, because we all enjoy doing things—like living.

Donny has a lot in common with our math teacher. They've both been in the seventh grade for the past three years. Not that that's bad, but Donny loves to scare the younger kids by doing things like flexing his muscles or growing a beard.

Anyway, after Donny pushed me up against the locker, I quickly bounced back, looked Donny right in the eyes, and shouted, "Look, you big bully, you can't push me like that!"

Okay, those weren't my *exact* words. And I didn't actually stare him in the eyes. It was more like his stomach, because Donny's about two feet taller than me. And what I really said was, "OW!" But he knew what I meant.

That was when Clay, who loves to watch people fight, shouted, "Are you going to let Donny push you around like a wimp?"

"Uh . . . yeah," I said, wondering when exactly Clay went blind and forgot how big Donny was.

Then I decided that I needed to stand up for myself, so I mumbled, "You shouldn't push me, Donny."

Donny replied with a witty "Huh?" and poked me in the shoulder with a finger the size of a banana. Now, I don't mind having a pierced shoulder—maybe the look will catch on—but Donny quickly followed up his poke by shoving me across the hall.

Now *that* was going too far. I jumped up and rushed at him with all my strength. *BAM!* A sad, whimpering cry filled the school. Unfortunately, the whimper was mine. To understand how I felt, try this: Put down this book and run into a wall. (Hurts, doesn't it?)

The only part of fighting I'm good at is the falling down part. Last year I took one karate lesson; it didn't go too well. First, I look terrible in pajamas. Second, I have extremely ticklish feet. I tried to kick my opponent in the chest, but my karate scream came out, "Hiya-hee-hee-hee!"

My opponent was Pat, a kid from my class. If he stood next to me, we'd look like the number 10. Kids pick on him because he's overweight and smells really bad. I think the karate teacher made us partners to build Pat's self-confidence.

Back to me versus Donny. Obviously I'm not a fighter, but he and I were in a battle. I did pretty well avoiding him. Then I started mixing things up by pounding Donny's fist several times with my face. Finally, he hit me right in the nose, and it started bleeding.

Now, I didn't cry (because I'm a man), but I got something in my eyes that made them water. I think it might've been Donny's fist. I fell to the ground, using up my one good fighting move, and Donny moved in to finish me off.

I started praying for God to supernaturally beam Donny out to the playground—and to make me wiser so I wouldn't be stupid enough to get in a fight in the future. But for now, I was preparing to suffer. All of a sudden, I saw a blinding flash knock Donny against the wall. He slithered away, and I was saved!

I looked up to see Pat holding out his hand to help me up. I couldn't believe it. Pat wasn't my friend. He wasn't *anyone's* friend, but he rescued me!

"Why did you do that?" I asked.

He grinned and said, "I'm a Christian, and, well, I want to be like Jesus. He would have helped you."

I was amazed—and terrified, because I saw the school's principal walking toward us. Mrs. Higginbotham quickly corralled me, Donny, and Pat into her office.

We all got in big trouble. The principal called all our parents and gave each of us a week of detention. Donny didn't mind; he already had an assigned seat waiting for him.

Pat and I decided to stick together. I think we'll become great friends (after we have some serious talks about when to shower and the new discoveries in deodorant).

I went to class feeling a little better about the whole situation—at least until my teacher asked for my math homework.

Super Average Advice

Bullying can be a pretty big problem. Four out of five students say they've been bullied at school. About half of all boys admit that they've been in a fight. (The other half probably can't admit it until the swelling goes down.)

The Bible doesn't talk specifically about bullies, but God's Word gives plenty of good ideas on how to handle the Donnys of the world.

Stay Away from trouble. Proverbs 27:12 says, "Wise people see danger and go to a safe place. But childish people keep on going and suffer for it" (NIrv). You don't have to be a genius to figure out who's a bully. Once you've identified the bullies in your school, do your best to stay away from them, especially when you're alone. Hanging out with a group of friends can help keep bullies at a distance.

Don't be afraid. Bullies, just like some wild animals, sense fear. With the Supreme Power in the

Did You Know?

- The most bullying takes place in sixth through eighth grades.
- Every seven minutes a child is bullied in the U.S.
- All bullies pick their noses.
  Note: Only two of these three facts can be proved.

universe living inside you, you don't have to be afraid. According to Deuteronomy 20:4 (ESV), "The Lord your God is he who goes with you to fight for you against your enemies, to give you the victory"! That doesn't mean God's going to bash every bully upside the head. Instead He'll show you how to fight the right way. Jesus never punched anybody, but He gained everybody's respect—even His enemies'—with the way He lived. Try to follow Jesus' example of standing for the truth and showing love to everybody.

Reach out. Many times, bullies pick on other kids because they feel bad about themselves. What they need is a friend. Maybe you could get a buddy or two (there's strength and safety in numbers) and eat lunch with a bully. Buy him a soda. Offer to help with homework. Jesus said to "love your enemies and pray for those who persecute you" (Matthew 5:44). If the bully accepts your friendship, you've got yourself one powerful pal. If he or she dumps your lunch on your lap, you can still be happy knowing you've shown someone Christ's love. Just pray that your mom feels the same way when she's washing ketchup out of your hoodie.

GOD'S GUIDE

Read: 1 Peter 3:9-13
- Think about a time when you repaid evil with a blessing.
- How do these verses make you feel about bullies? How should you treat them? How does God feel toward people who do evil?

_____

_____

_____

_____

_____

_____

_____

BONUS QUESTION

Do you use deodorant and if so, what flavor is it?

_____

4

How does God pick our parents? I know He *always* knows what He's doing, but sometimes my parents seem a little weird.

For instance, my dad is a history nut. When he's not watching some show on the Learning Channel about an ancient war between two countries that don't even exist anymore such as Australasia or France, he's turning our family vacations into educational "field trips." We usually end up at an old battlefield where we stand around as Dad tells us what happened there in 1820. This always inspires me to ask patriotic questions such as, "Does our hotel have a pool?"

My dad is also a prank master. He constantly pulls pranks on me. The first one took place when he told me to meet him somewhere, and then he didn't show up.

I remember calling him and saying, "Dad, I'm in Arkansas like you said. By the way, the map you gave me was for Montana—but I found an Arkansas map at one of the bus stops. Anyway, where are you?"

"Still at home in Texas!" he said. "Gotcha!"

Man, he had a good laugh about that—until he got the bill from Greyhound Bus.

My dad and I love to tease each other. In fact, I once wrote in my diary, "The day my dad *doesn't* try to pull a prank on me is about as likely to happen as my dad saying, 'No, thank you. Two doughnuts are enough.'"

The worst prank my dad ever pulled on me happened last year. I showed up at school wearing a pink bunny outfit only to discover that everyone else was dressed in normal clothes. It was not "Pink Bunny Outfit Day," like Dad had said. In fact, there isn't even a "Pink Bunny Outfit Day" on the calendar.

Three days later my Dad locked me out of the house during a snowstorm.

"Who is it?" my dad asked as I banged on the door.

"Your favorite son!" I replied.

"How can that be?" he said. "Your brother's right here by the toasty-warm fireplace!"

"Come on, Dad!" I whined. "Let me in!"

"No, thank you," he answered. "Two dough-nuts *are* enough!"

I made a mental note right then to start locking up my diary.

Mom has some quirks, too, like always having to go to the bathroom. I think she was born with a hummingbird's bladder instead of a normal human one. During car trips, this drives my dad crazy. Every time we pull back on the highway after a visit to a gas station, he says, "The next rest stop isn't for another four miles. Let's all try to make it!"

Don't get me wrong. I love my parents. It's just that we don't always get along perfectly.

But I know the book of Ephesians says to honor your father and mother. So one day after I didn't listen to my dad (a big fly was buzzing around the whole time he was talking), I decided to take my family to the zoo. I wanted to say I was sorry and show my love for them. Plus, I wanted to go to the zoo.

I had no idea the zoo cost $12 a person! That's $48! For $48, I expected the animals to do more than just sit there. For $48, I wanted to see a lion eat a guy. Not really, but $48 is a lot of money to spend watching sleeping animals.

Not only did the animals snooze the whole time, but I was insulted at the gift shop. My dad wanted to buy me a hat as a souvenir for being so

Did You Know?

- Parents spend well over $160,000 to raise a child.
- People in Utah have the most children—averaging 2.21 per family. West Virginians have the least number of children in the United States: 1.71.
- Parent spelled backwards is Tnerap, which is the Greek word for "rules with a hairy fist." *

* You may want to check a Greek dictionary before you believe everything you read.

thoughtful. A girl walked up and said, "Can I help you?"

"I'm looking for a hat," I said.

She looked at my hair and said, "Duh. Why'd you wait so long?!"

What does that mean? I have great hair even though my dad says it looks like I comb it with an eggbeater.

On the way home from the zoo, Mom said that it was the best day ever because her son did something really nice for her. Then she asked if Dad could pull off at the next gas station for a bathroom break.

It quickly became my best day ever, too. I felt good seeing my parents happy because of something I did.

As I was sitting in the backseat feeling all happy, my dad said, "Uh, Bob, could you put your hat back on? Birds are circling the car, trying to nest on your head."

Super Average Advice

Parents are like noses. Everybody's got 'em, and it's not a good idea to pick at them. But some kids feel like their parents are always picking *on* them.

"Clean your room."

"Finish your homework."

"Get down from that ceiling fan!"

"Chew with your mouth closed."

"Take out the trash."

"Watch your attitude."

"Brush your teeth before you go to church."

A parent's requests can be numerous. The next time you start feeling overwhelmed by your parents' expectations, take a moment to:

Put yourself in their shoes. Parents have a huge responsibility. Psalm 127:3 (NIrV) says, "Children are a gift from the Lord." If God gives you something, you want to take good care of it. That means parents should take feeding, clothing, educating, and nurturing their children pretty seriously. But parents aren't responsible just for your physical needs. They provide for your emotional and spiritual needs as well. If you know Jesus Christ personally, can you remember who introduced the two of you? A parent probably had something to do with the most important decision you'll ever make: to follow Jesus.

Parents want the best for you, even when they discipline you or take away privileges. Their advice and rules may sound like nagging but they know their time with you is short (18 years may not feel that way—but compared with eternity, it is) so they want to teach you as much as they can. Plus, they want to make sure what they're teaching is sticking to your brain.

Think about the future. The adult you become directly reflects on your parents. As you get older, you'll probably notice that your sense of humor, personality, and even the way you look have a lot to do with your parents. Family is forever. Developing a good relationship with your parents now, which includes good communication and understanding, will pay off big-time as you grow. If you feel a rule is unfair, tell them. When you want help with an important decision, ask them. Parents want to be a huge part of your life. The more you communicate, the closer you'll become.

God's Guide

Read: Proverbs 23:22-25 and Philippians 2:14-15
- What are some ways you could make your parents happy?
- How do you think your parents feel when you complain about one of their rules? How does God want you to act? When you obey your parents, who might notice your actions?

_____

_____

_____

_____

_____

Bonus Question

Do you know how to repair a ceiling fan?

5

I don't like to brag—which works out well because I'm not really great at doing anything, especially sports.

Last week we raced around the track in P.E. I was at a full sprint when a butterfly actually landed on me. How embarrassing! I lost my concentration and came in last. I thought I might beat Rebecca because she broke her leg, but that girl can really work those crutches.

Not being athletically gifted doesn't stop me from playing sports, like my favorite one: kickball. If you don't know what kickball is, I'll try to explain. It's like baseball only with a big bouncy ball that you kick, instead of hit with a bat. The pitcher rolls the ball toward home plate, and the kicker kicks it—or in my case, doesn't. I might be the only person in the history of kickball to strike out.

But it's not totally my fault. I think my school uses the first kickball ever created. A big "Vote for George Washington" sticker is stuck on it. Also, it's not really round, so it rolls funny. Several dents make it look like it got in a fight with some tough soccer balls. They make it bounce in strange directions, especially when it bounces off my face— which it does anytime I try to catch it.

I've never been good at catching anything, except the flu, which is why I play the outfield. Actually my team puts me outside the outfield— way back in the parking lot. I usually bring a book to keep me occupied. When it's time for my team to kick, they signal me by shooting flares into the air. Then I get on my bike and ride in to meet the rest of the team.

One day I'm hoping to get good enough to play the infield. My dad and I work out at a gym, so I will get stronger and more athletic. Dad is up to 30 minutes on the treadmill! I also use the treadmill, but I actually turn it on and run on it. Every day I speed it up so I can get in better shape. Yesterday I went up to five, which was so fast I almost dropped my jelly doughnut.

My gym membership came with five free sessions with one of the personal trainers. I knew God placed me with the perfect trainer because as I approached the desk, they all instantly walked off but one. She was reading a book. When she looked up, I showed her my free training coupons and she couldn't contain her excitement.

"Oh, goody," she said.

She took out a clipboard and asked me what my goals were. I told her that I wanted to become the world's best kickball player and build the body of a professional football player. She looked at me and said, "Uh . . . we'd better get started."

We went over to the bench press. "What's your max?" she asked.

I answered "105," because that's the most I've ever weighed.

"Really?" she asked, wrinkling her forehead. She placed a gigantic disc on each end of the bar.

"Do three sets of 10," she said.

The weights were big but I knew I could handle them because I'm not just anyone—I'm Average Boy!

I laid down on the bench, grabbed the bar, and . . . you know how it's called "the bench press"? Well,

Did You Know?

- By age 13, nearly three out of four kids have stopped playing organized sports.
- Playing sports makes you dumb, because all the blood rushes to your muscles—not your brain.*
- Watching 30 minutes of TV burns about 30 calories. Half an hour of skateboarding works off 115 calories—not even counting the calories you burn as you rush to the emergency room. Playing basketball burns 175 calories. And 30 minutes of swimming destroys a whopping 260 calories. What do you think is best for your body?

* Don't try saying this to any jocks.

they should actually call it "the chest smash."

Never before had I been so aware of gravity as when that bar came smashing down on my chest. The wind was instantly knocked out of me. My personal trainer quickly knelt down and looked under the bench.

"I don't think the bar went all the way through," I squeaked.

"It's not that," she said. "I'm looking for the

little girl who just screamed."

Well, that happened a couple of days ago but I am not giving up. I'm continuing to work out because I know God wants us to strengthen our bodies and our minds. You never know when He will give us a chance to do something great, and we have to be in shape to take it on.

That's why I'm sticking with this workout thing. Now I'm able to do three sets of 10 on the bench press! If I keep this up, my trainer says we'll eventually put some weight back on the bar. However, if we do that, I might have to set down my jelly doughnut.

Super Average Advice

Sports are fun, as along as you don't mind scrapes, sprains, bruises, and broken bones. Just kidding. They can also be a great way to take care of your body. Experts suggest doing 30 to 60 minutes of exercise every day. But statistics show that 25 percent of kids get less than 30 minutes of physical activity a day.

The apostle Paul wrote most of the books in the New Testament. He talked a lot about sports and maintaining a strong body. By using some of Paul's ideas, you can learn a lot about athletics.

Try your best. Doing well in sports takes practice and maximum effort. Check out what Paul wrote in 1 Corinthians 9:24-27 (NIrV). He starts off that section of Scripture saying only one person gets the prize in a race, so "run in a way that will get you the prize." Then he ends by adding, "I train my body and bring it under control."

Proper training leads to success. You have to work your body hard to grow stronger. Winning is nice, but it's not the ultimate goal. When you "do your best to get the prize," that means playing by the rules, obeying the coach, improving on the abilities God gave you, and giving your all—in practice and in games.

God's not done with you yet. Don't let past flops prevent you from jumping back into a sport or trying a new activity in the future. Over the next few years, you'll probably grow a lot physically, spiritually, and mentally. Some of the best athletes are late bloomers. David Robinson, a former National Basketball Association Most Valuable Player, world champion, and multiple gold medalist, played only one year of high school basketball. But then he grew seven inches at the Naval Academy. Michael Jordan, possibly the best basketball player of all time, got cut from his high school team during his sophomore year.

The apostle Paul says, "I've got my eye on the

goal, where God is beckoning us onward—to Jesus. I'm off and running, and I'm not turning back" (Philippians 3:13-14, MSG). So look ahead, dream big dreams, and keep your eyes focused on Christ.

God's Guide

Read: 1 Timothy 4:7-9
- Think about ways you can train yourself to become more godly.
- Does God think working out and having a strong body are important? What's more important in His opinion: training in godliness or physical training? How will you use this fact to adjust the ways you spend your time?

_____

_____

_____

Bonus Tip

Don't do chin-ups on the bar bolted to the wall right by the gym door. That's actually there for coats and hats. If you do try this, people will look at you funny.

THE COST OF BEING COOL

6

It's great to have a ton of friends. When I walk through the hallways at school, kids greet me left and right.

"Hey, Mark!"

"Yo, Timmy!"

"What up, Jim!"

Even though they say the wrong name, I know they know who I am! I have tons of friends.

I think that's why I always get picked last for kickball. The captains know I'm sure to get picked because of my popularity. So they pick the other kids first. I sit in the back and smile, trying not to feel bad for the unpopular kids as they walk to their teams.

Wanting friends can be dangerous, however. You shouldn't let the quest for popularity make you do something you know is wrong. I'll give you an example.

Clint and Chris are two of the most popular guys at my school. Clint is cool because he has a leather jacket that smells like a real cow! The teacher says it smells like a real *dead* cow, but we all know it's cool. So does Clint. He never takes it off. Come to think of it, maybe he can't because the cowhide has glued itself to his skin. He's had it on for the two years I've known him. If he ever does try to take it off, I don't want to be around.

Chris, on the other hand, is cool because he's the best-looking kid in the class. Girls like him almost as much as he likes himself.

One day we were going through the lunch line and Chris said, "Hey, Brad."

"Hey, Chris," I said, "I go by Bob now because that's my name."

"Whatever," Chris answered. "Want to be friends with Clint and me?"

"Sure!" I said getting very excited. "But can I sit next to you and not Clint? I can't eat with the smell of dead cow in the air."

"Yeah," Chris said coolly. "But we need you to do something as our friend. Can you get us some chocolate milk?"

I had only enough money for my lunch, so this was a problem. But Clint had a plan. The lunch lady sat between the cash register and this big square ice-box behind her that held the milk. After someone paid her for lunch, she would open the chest and hand him a milk carton.

That's when Clint wanted me to sneak behind the other side of the icebox. When the lunch lady opened up the lid and turned to hand the next kid some milk, I was supposed to reach in and grab two chocolate milks.

"That's stealing!" I said.

"Come on," Chris said. "We'll be your friends. You can even be in our band. Do you play an instrument?"

The thought of playing my triangle in a rock band was very tempting, but I knew it was wrong to steal.

"You'll be really popular," Clint added.

I don't know if it was his compelling argument or the dead cow smell making me dizzy (I could have sworn that Clint's jacket actually mooed at me!), but I decided to do it. I snuck around the ice chest. Just like at our school dance, no one noticed me. I was hiding behind it when I heard Donny say, "I'll take a chocolate milk."

"Same as the last four years," the lunch lady said. "One chocolate milk for the only kid in school old enough to vote!"

The lunch lady has a mean sense of humor. However, I didn't have time to think about that. My heart raced like crazy. The icebox lid opened. I heard the lunch lady grab the milk and turn. I reached around and grabbed two milks. That's when the icebox lid crashed down on my arm!

"*Auuuggghhhhhh!*" I screamed, flopping around like my friend Billy the time he got his tongue stuck

Did You Know?

A Time/Nickelodeon survey of kids ages 9 to 14 found:
- 36 percent of middle schoolers feel pressure from peers to steal things from stores.
- 40 percent get pressured to drink alcohol.
- 80 percent of tweens feel extreme pressure from friends to stand on their chair in the cafeteria and sing, "I'm a little teapot."

Fact: One of these three statistics might be made up.

to the freezer door.

The lunch lady turned and said, "What in the world are you doing, Ben?"

"I go by Bob now, and I'm working on a new dance move," I said, trying to hide the fact that my arm was still stuck in the icebox.

"Are you stealing milk?" she said.

"Uh, yes, ma'am," I said, dropping my head to match my sinking heart.

She opened the lid. I had lost most of the feeling in my arm, so I didn't realize my hand still clutched the two milk cartons.

"You were stealing skim milk?" the lunch lady said, laughing. "No one drinks skim milk. Those two cartons have been in there since the day I started working here!"

Not only did I find out that I'm a bad thief, but I learned a great lesson about hanging out with the wrong crowd. It doesn't matter if kids think I'm cool if I'm not being myself.

I decided right then that I wasn't going to let other kids pressure me into doing stuff I knew was wrong. Besides, doing bad things to gain friends isn't worth it, because I already have a great best friend: Jesus. He is the only friend that matters. Jesus will be with me after I'm out of school. He will be with me after I leave this world. Clint and

Chris didn't apologize, and they weren't my friends after that, which was fine with me. Jesus is the only friend I really need.

Super Average Advice

Peer pressure often makes kids do things they wouldn't normally do—both bad and good.

Bad peer pressure could influence you to watch a movie you know you shouldn't, sneak over to a friend's house, drink alcohol, or steal milk. Good peer pressure can encourage you to stand up for a kid who's being picked on, finish your homework, walk closer to Jesus, say no to drugs, or brush your sister's hair (all right, the hair thing may be going too far). The trick to deciding what kind of pressure you're under is to look at your friends.

Know your friends. If your friends always get in trouble at home and at school, they probably pull you in a bad direction. On the other hand, if your friends take school seriously, show respect for authority, and try their best to follow Jesus, then they can be good influences on your life. The book of Proverbs contains tons of wisdom, and it says this about the people you hang out with: "He who walks with the wise grows wise, but a companion of fools suffers harm" (13:20). So it's not cool to be a fool—unless you enjoy being in trouble. Be wise and win the prize. (The rhyming will stop now. *Sorry.*)

Follow your ultimate Friend. Jesus created you with unique talents and gifts. One of the best ways to honor your Creator is to be yourself. If hanging out with a certain group of kids causes you to say things you normally wouldn't say or dress inappropriately, they're pulling you away from who you are. If you like Christian music instead of heavy metal rock, that's cool! If you prefer to wear T-shirts instead of tank tops—awesome.

We're all created in God's image. And God gave us the perfect example to follow. In John 13:15, Jesus says, "I have set you an example that you should do as I have done for you." Jesus wasn't caught up trying to hang out with the cool people. In fact, He ignored peer pressure and did God's will for His life. And that's something worth following.

BONUS TIP

Playing air-triangle in the car is fun, but not in church. If you make the preacher laugh, you'll get in trouble.

Read: 1 Corinthians 15:33-34

- Do you hang out with any friends who pull you away from God? What could you do to get out of that situation? Is it time to make some new friends?
- Write down some ways you can encourage your friends to follow God.

_____

_____

_____

_____

_____

_____

_____

7

I love my brother and have always been there for him. I helped carry him into the house after we discovered our Big Wheel couldn't fly. I was there to shout encouragement when he jumped off the top bunk and got smacked in the head by the ceiling fan.

He took forever to stagger out of his room holding his head. I kept encouraging him by shouting phrases like, "The bleeding's slowing down. Keep up that pressure. You're doing great!" and "Nobody will ever notice the scar, if you always wear a hat." Yup, I'm always there for my little brother.

One day we were sitting in church. The preacher was giving this really long prayer. I had my head down, and I started rubbing my eyes, which sounded like this: *SPPLLLOOCHHH-TAATAALOONCHY.* I didn't know that when you rub your eyes really hard, everyone around you can hear that popping-squishy sound. I thought it was just a noise inside my head. My dad looked up and whispered, "Bob, stop!"

"What?" I whispered back.

He silently mouthed the words, "You need to learn how to act in church."

I've never been really good at lipreading, so I thought he said, "You need to act in church."

I always try to obey my parents. So I jumped into action!

I quickly ran to the front of the church and started reciting a monologue from a play I had recently starred in. I ran the curtain for that play, which is the most important part of a good drama, but it had very few lines. So I tried to recite some of the other actors' lines.

"To be or not to be . . . uh . . . that's a toughy," I said.

"Meet me outside!" my dad added, joining my monologue.

If only he would've talked that loud to begin

with, I wouldn't have been in trouble. Anyway, 20 minutes later I was back in our pew sitting next to my brother. I had a songbook on my lap and was sitting very quietly. That's when I noticed a fly had landed on my brother's head. One of my jobs as an older brother is to protect my siblings. However, I also know that I shouldn't talk in church.

That's when I remembered the songbook on my lap. Looking back, I may have swung the book a little too hard. But in my defense, the fly was gone. Of course, so was I.

After knocking the fly off my brother's head, I quickly tried to help him up off the floor. My dad used to play sports and is still pretty quick and strong. He picked me up and carried me like a football toward the back of the church. I tried to grab stuff to slow him down. Before I knew it, I had two pencils, our church bulletin, a Bible, and Mrs. Ray's glasses.

At one point, my dad looked back and saw my hands full of stuff.

"PUT THOSE THINGS DOWN!" he whispered quietly enough that people in other churches probably couldn't hear him.

"I haven't filled out our attendance card yet," I said.

"Trust me," he "whispered" again. "Everybody

knows we were here today."

Once we were outside, I dropped the items and my dad dropped me. Soon my brother and mom joined us. I told my family how I was protecting my brother. He said he would've preferred to take his chances with the fly.

My dad then asked my brother to make a list of ways I could be a good brother. I was amazed at some of the things on the list. For one, he wanted me to ask him to play when Billy came over. He also asked me to stay out of his room, especially at night when he's trying to sleep. I guess he doesn't like being scared awake.

Another thing my brother wanted was to go fishing with me, and other stuff I didn't think he liked doing. I've been trying to do the things on his list lately, and we're having a lot of fun together!

Basically, being a good brother is just being a good Christian friend. If you act like a friend toward your siblings, you'll get in less trouble. Not to mention you'll gain an extra friend!

Now if you will excuse me, my brother and I are going to go sneak in and scare my dad while he's sleeping. It's great having a new friend to do stuff with.

Super Average Advice

Siblings have been getting on each other's nerves since the beginning of time. Even with the whole world at their feet, the first two siblings set a very bad example about brotherly love.

Who can forget what happened when Cain said to Abel, "Hey, bro, come check out this gigantic corn I grew. It's wearing some huge earphones." Abel followed his brother into the field, but only Cain came back (Genesis 4:8).

Hopefully, things haven't gotten that bad at

Did You Know?

- Brothers and sisters fight because they're bored, tired, or hungry, want attention, are annoyed at each other, or _____ (insert your answer here).
- Sibling rivalry happens in large families with more than 20 kids and small families with only two children.
- One way to settle a fight with a brother is to play "Rock, Paper, Scissors."
  Note: Don't use actual rocks, paper, and scissors!

your house. But if you have a brother or sister, chances are sparks will fly. When you spend a lot of time together, even little things can become annoying. Maybe you don't like how your sibling eats, messes with your stuff, teases you, hits you, gets away with things, or breathes. Some siblings fight over the silliest things.

Sarah: Gross, Seth, why can't you eat normal? That sloppy joe coming out of your mouth looks like blood.

Seth: You mean you don't like "see food"? *Aaauuuauau. (Add yucky, spinning tongue motion here.)*

Other times disputes can be serious. If your sibling hits or kicks you, talk to a parent. Also, privacy issues like reading your secret diary or walking into your room without knocking can cause big problems.

But while your brothers or sisters may bother you, you'll have to admit that deep down inside you love them. Love is the key to sibling relationships because family is for life.

Siblings stick together. King Solomon knew something about family life. He's considered one of the wisest and most powerful kings in the Bible, and he had 700 wives. (Even he would probably admit that wasn't a great idea because that's 700 mothers-in-law!) Solomon wrote in Proverbs 17:17

(NKJV), "A friend loves at all times, and a brother is born for adversity." That means when times are tough, you should be the first one to help out, say a kind word, and stand up for anyone who needs support. This goes for your elementary, middle school, and junior high years, and way beyond!

Try these ideas for getting along with your siblings:

Focus on the positives. If your sister sings all the time, encourage her talent. But you can also let her know that your ear doesn't make a good microphone!

Be happy for each other. Parents can't give their children an equal amount of attention all the time. Sometimes your siblings will get extra time with Mom or Dad. Maybe your sister will get straight *A*s or your brother will win a contest. Instead of being jealous, share in their joy.

Find some free time. Even if you love your siblings to death, every once in a while you'll need some space. When your nerves wear thin, tell your brother or sister that you want to do something by yourself but can play with him or her later.

GOD'S GUIDE

Read: Galatians 6:9-10

- Write down some nice things you can do for the people in your life.
- If God wants you to be nice to everybody, especially those in the "family of believers," how do you think He'd want you to treat your brothers and sisters who may be family *and* Christians?

_____

_____

_____

_____

BONUS ACTIVITY

Test your brother's reflexes by hiding in a dark room and jumping out to surprise him. Just make sure he's not carrying something that could spill or break at the time, because things could get messy!

I've got a beard! Technically, it's just two hairs on my chin. But in the right light and from the right angle, it looks like a full beard.

My dad says it looks like I have some sort of disease. He enjoys pointing out that you can't call it a beard until you're able to see the whiskers from more than six inches away. I think he's just in denial because it's obviously a thick, manly, two-whisker beard. In fact, I plan to wear a flannel shirt and hang out with lumberjacks by the end of the week!

My body is going through other changes as well. For instance, my voice is getting deeper. For the longest time people who called on the phone would say, "Hey, little girl, is your mommy or daddy home?" But with my new deeper voice coming in, that's starting to change. Today when I answered the phone, the man said, "Excuse me, ma'am, are you the lady of the house?"

Ha! Did you hear that? "Ma'am!" He obviously mistook me for a much older girl. I sure wish he could have seen me in person, so he would've seen my beard. Maybe he would've even thought I was a grandmother!

Anyway, I'm glad my voice has finally settled down to a manly tenor pitch. For about a month, my voice would crack and go from super high to amazingly low. It sounded like Mickey Mouse and Darth Vader trying to say a sentence at the same time.

I didn't mind because everyone's body goes through changes. My dad claims that he once looked like me. Of course, I'm guessing that was before he was born. My dad was born big. In fact, I'm pretty sure he was born on a Thursday and a Friday—with a beard. But he still claims he was skinny and very, very short until age 12.

"Then I shot straight up!" my dad says.

"And straight out," my mom likes to joke.

The point is, we all go through the changes of

puberty. It's as if around age 12 we all fall into a vat of toxic chemicals and our bodies quickly gain mutant superhero powers that allow us to grow pimples and armpit hair. (Hopefully, we'll choose to use our powers for good, not evil!) I'm excited about the changes, because they remind me that I'm growing into the person God wants me to be.

Speaking of massive growth, my bicep muscles are getting huge! Just yesterday my mom needed help opening a jar of mayonnaise. While my grandmother opened it for her, Mom commented on how she thought I looked more muscular.

"You almost opened the jar this time," she said.

"Thanks, I've been working out," I gloated. "I do six push-ups a day."

"Wow, that's a lot," she said in amazement.

"Well, not in a row," I admitted.

Having muscles is fun. I've always been superskinny. But with my muscles starting to grow, I was thinking I'd go as a bodybuilder to this year's Fall Festival.

"A bodybuilder?" my dad said when I told him my plan. "Maybe you should go as a marathon runner instead."

He's just jealous because he's not the only muscle man in the house now.

Hey, my brother just walked into my room and

slipped on the floor. This reminds me of one more change I'm going through. My hair and face can now produce massive amounts of oil. This is great because I'm always hearing about how the world is running out of oil. Not at my house! In fact, I should put together a proposal where the U.S. government starts paying 12-year-olds for the oil found on our combs every morning.

It would solve our oil shortage, and I wouldn't have to mow lawns for money every summer. The president will be so happy that a kid from Texas solved the oil shortage. Well, maybe I'll wait to send my proposal until I'm done building my rocket ship to help out NASA.

Anyway, we all have different shapes and body styles because God is very creative and gives us all His own touch of originality. As your body goes through changes, don't let other kids make you feel embarrassed. Everybody hits his or her growth spurt at a different time. Remember that God is shaping and molding us into unique superheroes, each one with special talents.

Now if you'll excuse me, my dad wants Beardman to use his talents to mow the lawn. I can't wait to start selling oil to the government!

Super Average Advice

"Change is good." That would be the perfect slogan for growing up, although all the changes don't sound too good.

Most people would probably prefer *not* to:

• endure crazy growth spurts (sometimes shooting up several inches in a summer);

• hear their voices crack and squeak;

• have hair growing in places where it didn't before;

• start *needing* to shower every day and wear deodorant;

• watch their body shape change;

• battle blemishes.

But believe it or not, these aches, pains, and embarrassing happenings are all worth it in the end. (Don't believe it? Just ask your parents.)

If these changes haven't already started happening to you, they soon will. Puberty is a natural and necessary part of growing up, and it affects boys and girls differently. However, there are a couple of things you can remember that will help you get through this wild time of change.

God is in control. He already knows what you'll look like as an adult. Psalm 139:13-14 says, "For you created my inmost being; you knit me together in my mother's womb. I praise you

- Girls can begin growing much taller at age 8, two years before boys. But boys typically don't stop growing until they're 16—two years after girls have their biggest growth spurt.
- Getting lots of sleep during the tween years is important, because that's when you grow the most.
- The hairiest man in the world was born with 96 percent of his body covered in hair.*

* That's actually true! Check out www.guinness worldrecords.com.

because I am fearfully and wonderfully made; your works are wonderful." You may feel like your legs are too long or your face is too round, but God's not done with you yet.

The roller-coaster ride will end. All this growing, stretching, and changing is tiring. Your body will ache. You may notice that you're more moody or you get angry more quickly. While that's natural, don't let it be an excuse for you to give in to your emotions and make life miserable for the people around you.

The prophet Isaiah wasn't necessarily talking about puberty, but his words in Isaiah 40:30-31 can help you when you're feeling weak and depressed: "Even youths grow tired and weary, and young men stumble and fall; but those who hope in the LORD will renew their strength. They will soar on wings like eagles; they will run and not grow weary, they will walk and not be faint." Hang in there and trust God. He always knows what He's doing. And He'll give you the strength to make it through anything—including puberty!

GOD'S GUIDE

Read: Luke 2:52

- Jesus was 100 percent man and 100 percent God. He had to go through the same changes you do. Because Jesus is your ultimate example and the One you follow, write down some ways that you want to grow "in wisdom and stature, and in favor with God and men."

_____

_____

_____

_____

If you could have any kind of superhero power,
what would it be?

9

Today in science class we went to a creek behind our school to identify different kinds of funguses (also called fungi, according to the teacher). I told our teacher we could do the same thing in the lunchroom by observing the food on our trays. He just reminded me to put the protective glasses over my eyes and the protective duct tape over my mouth.

By the way, I don't think it's fair that I'm the only one who has to put duct tape over his mouth every time we do an experiment. The teacher should care about the other students' safety, too! But

I've always been the class favorite, so I'm used to special treatment.

Once we got to the creek, the teacher explained the lab—which is not a type of loyal, friendly dog. (Science is so confusing!) This kind of lab requires us to get our hands dirty. The teacher wanted us to collect funguses. Well, I play at this creek every day after school, so I know where all the funguses are. My dad says most of them live between my toes, but I know they really like to be under rocks.

Speaking of rocks, I also know where all the big rocks are located just under the water. I went to a deep part of the creek that had seven big rocks submerged just under the surface. By walking on these rocks, I can make it look like I'm standing on the water. I leaped off the bank and jumped from rock to rock until I was in the middle of the stream. Then I ripped off the duct tape and yelled, "Hey, Donny! Bet you can't catch me!"

Donny instantly jumped up, ran into the creek, and disappeared into the murky water. He bobbed up and started swimming toward me as fast as he could.

I quickly offered him some encouragement. "Don't forget to gather some funguses!" I should've yelled, "Donny, you're about to swim into a rock!" He smashed into a rock, but he did

get some funguses—on his forehead.

Our teacher shouted, "Donny, out of that water! Bob, put that tape back over your mouth!" The teacher was so mad, he immediately took us inside and gave us a pop quiz.

I usually don't do too well on tests. Maybe it's because when I hear the word *test*, my hands start shaking, my heart starts pounding, and my body starts sweating like crazy. (The same thing happens when I try to talk to a girl.)

I was so nervous that I froze on the first question. I had no idea what the answer was. I kept telling myself, *Just stay calm. You know this. You've studied it. Just reread the question.* So I did.

"Name: _____"

Nothing came to my mind!

Fortunately, the teacher said, "Bob, are you having some trouble starting?"

I grinned and said, "Not anymore!"

Once I got the answer to "Name" correct, the rest of the quiz was a breeze. I just did what I always do on multiple-choice tests: Answer every question with a *b*. This saves me a lot of time and brainpower. Plus, I love writing *b* because I have two of them in my first name.

While I'm not that great at tests, I am pretty good at spelling. This year I won our class spelling bee! Donny got out in the first round. I kind of felt responsible. His word was *shoe*. Right after he said "S," I accidentally sneezed. My *Achoo!* sounded like Donny saying "H-U." Oh well, the agony of defeat (and allergies) is all part of competition.

I flew through the first three rounds. *Trumpet* was my first word. I knew that one, because one summer I had to write, "I will not bring a trumpet on a long car trip" 100 times after our vacation. My next two words were *hamster* and *ambulance*. Past experiences have taught me those words as well. I'm sure glad Dad makes me write all those sentences!

Did You Know?

The best way to do well in school is to:
- concentrate in class;
- take notes on what the teacher says and what you read;
- ask your teacher questions about the stuff you don't understand;
- review your notes several consecutive nights before a test;
- Write all the answers on the inside of your eyelids.*

* Just don't use permanent ink unless you plan on taking the same test your entire life!

The final round came down to me and a girl we call Julie-the-Greatest-Speller-in-the-World. I think her real name is Mary. Things didn't look good for me, but to everyone's shock, she mis-spelled *guitar.* I quickly stood up, knowing if I got this word right, I'd win. The teacher said, "Forgiven."

Forgiven?

I knew this one! I had read it in the Bible many times. Because I believe in Jesus, I'm forgiven by God for all the times I mess up.

"F-O-R-G-I-V-E-N. Forgiven!" I shouted.

"That's correct," my teacher said.

It was the first time I'd ever won anything in school—unless you count the time my fourth-grade teacher gave me a lifetime pass to the princi-pal's office.

Super Average Advice

Let's get one thing straight: Tests aren't fun. (No surprise there, right?) In fact, they can be kind of scary. If you don't do well, you could:

- get bad grades on your report card;
- never get into an Ivy League college;
- be forced to sit in the corner of the classroom with a traffic cone on your head;
- end up living in a van by a large body of water.

All right, maybe the consequences aren't that bad. Most kids want to do well on tests. Many have the correct information crammed in their brains next to a bunch of song lyrics and a recipe for the ultimate banana split. The problem is brain freeze, or what might be called test anxiety.

The best way to conquer this problem is to face it head-on.

Step One: Fight Fear. God doesn't want you to be afraid: "The LORD is with me; I will not be afraid. What can man do to me? The LORD is with me; he is my helper. I will look in triumph on my enemies" (Psalm 118:6-7).

Just to make things clear. Your teachers (especially if you're homeschooled) are not your enemy. Tests are not the enemy. The point is, God is with you. And because the Creator of everything is on your side, you don't need to be afraid when test time comes.

Step Two: Flunk Failure. Who cares if you fail? God doesn't, but He does want you to put out maximum effort. Your worth in His eyes doesn't depend on good grades. God equally loves the straight-A student and the one who struggles.

Romans 5:8 says, "But God demonstrates his own love for us in this: While we were still sinners, Christ died for us." If God sacrificed His only Son for you despite all the bad stuff you do, certainly messing up on a test (even though you tried your hardest) won't bother Him. His love never changes. So use the mental gifts that God's given you and do your best on tests.

GOD'S GUIDE

Read: Colossians 3:23-24
- What does it mean to "work with all your heart"?
- If you're working for the Lord, do you think you will try harder or less hard? Why?
- How do these verses apply to schoolwork? Write out a plan that will help you do your best in school.

_____

_____

_____

_____

_____

_____

_____

Fungus can be found:

      b. on rocks;

      b. on trees;

      b. on Donny's head;

      b. between my toes.

10

Have you ever slept on your arm the wrong way? I woke up one morning and found my left arm completely asleep. It felt like it weighed about 100 pounds! Using my whole body, I flopped over my numb arm to hit the snooze alarm. I didn't feel a thing, but the music shut off.

Then I got out of bed and dropped a book on it—my hand, not my snooze alarm—although I've done that before, too. My arm felt so weird! I couldn't make it do anything. I started slinging my cold, lifeless arm around the room, banging it into stuff.

"What's all that noise?" my brother asked as he

walked into my room. "Are you beating yourself up? Can I help?"

"My arm's asleep, and I can't feel anything," I said. "Can you help me wake it up?"

I would like to point out that I said, "wake it up." I expected my brother to do something like scream, "Hey, arm. You've got work to do and cereal to shovel. Wake up!" I didn't expect that my brother would climb on my bed, jump into the air, and land on my hand—but that's exactly what he did.

At that point, my hand suddenly came back to life. It felt like a thousand tiny ants walking around and stinging my whole arm. I quickly pulled my hand out from under my brother and sent him flying into the wall.

"Auuuuugggghhhhh!" I screamed as I ran down the hallway. My half-numb arm whirled all over the place, banging off the hallway walls and sending pictures flying.

I ran into the living room. Actually, I ran into the coffee table, which was in the living room. "Awwwwwouuuuchhh!" I shouted. "Who put this coffee table here—where adults sometimes drink coffee? It's a bad place for it!"

Now my arm and leg both throbbed. I was so mad. I grabbed a football off the couch with my good arm and threw it at the coffee table. After all, the coffee table needed to be taught a lesson about hiding in the middle of the living room like that. The football bounced off the coffee table and straight up toward the ceiling fan.

My parents like to leave the ceiling fan going all the time. When the football hit the spinning blades, it soared right into the big glass mirror over the fireplace. I gasped and waited for a loud crashing noise.

Nothing. Not a sound. The football just bounced off the mirror and landed on the floor.

"Whew, that was a close one," I said.

That's when my brother tackled me.

"Get off me. I don't have the ball," I shouted. "Learn the rules to the game."

"You knocked the wind out of me when you pushed me!" my brother hollered.

"You nearly crushed every bone in my hand," I shouted back.

"Well, your arm is awake now, isn't it?" he replied.

I couldn't argue with that, so I yelled, "That was a dumb way to wake up my arm!"

My brother got even madder (he doesn't like to be called dumb), picked up the football, and threw it at me. Many times my superhero-like, lightning reflexes help me—this wasn't one of them. I ducked out of the way of the football only to hear the crashing noise I expected to hear the first time the football hit the mirror.

My dad came running out of the bathroom wearing an old white bathrobe, half-shaved, and with his hair messed up. He looked like a mad scientist! But when he saw the broken mirror, he just looked mad.

"What happened?" he shouted.

"Well, uh," I answered. "Hey, why do you always leave the ceiling fan on?"

Not only did my brother and I get in really bad trouble, we also had to pay for the glass and write a report on how the mirror got broken. My dad wanted us to retrace the steps that led to the bad results.

I was surprised by what I figured out. Several times, if I had stayed calm, it would've prevented the problem. If my brother or I had controlled our anger, the mirror wouldn't have been smashed.

Satan uses anger to get us to make bad decisions. (I believe Satan also uses coffee tables.) When you become angry, find ways to calm down before your anger gets you in trouble. I try to stop and pray when I'm feeling mad. Just talking to God helps.

Anyway, I hope you have an anger-free day.

Now if you will excuse me, I'm sitting funny in this chair and my arm is falling asleep again. I wonder how long it will take before it completely falls asllakjfoi nvck nsdkj nskvj nvkm,fc vkaerith8ouijlrjgkf v

Super Average Advice

Everybody gets angry. Even Jesus became angry when He saw people buying and selling things in the temple. He knocked over tables and drove away the merchants and money changers (Mark 11:15-16). The difference between Jesus' anger and our anger is that He didn't sin. His anger was righteous in defending God's house. Our anger is usually selfish as we defend ourselves.

Does this sound familiar? Your little sister takes something from your room without asking. You find her and rip *your* property out of her hands. She gets mad and stomps on your toe. You get even more angry and push her down. She gets angrier still and charges at you like a raging bull. You step out of the way and trip her so she falls into the couch. Mom comes into the room as your sister flies across the room and everybody gets into trouble. And that makes you the angriest, because *she* started it.

That's the problem with anger—it tends to escalate. Maybe you know what it's like to have anger bubbling inside you like molten lava gurgling under the earth's surface. Scientists say they can tell a volcano is about to erupt when it shakes and gives off gas. The same thing is true for people. They often shake and pass gas *(yuck!)* when they're angry. Before you explode with anger, try these eruption stoppers.

Blow off steam. Anger often brings a rush of energy and adrenaline. Put that energy into something positive by running around the block, riding your bike as fast as you can, tackling a giant teddy bear, throwing a football (outside), or banging on

Did You Know?

- Some people's faces can get really red when they're angry, which can actually be quite pretty (or scary, depending on the situation).
- School counselors are seeing an increase of anger and aggression in kids.
- People who get angry a lot are more likely to develop health problems, such as: headaches, high blood pressure, digestive problems, and heart disease.

some drums.

If you feel frustrated because somebody has wronged you and you want to get back at them, take a moment and pray to God. Tell Him your feelings. Let Him know that you're mad and want to get revenge. Then ask Him to help calm your emotions and trust Him to help you handle the situation. Remember what it says in Romans 12:19: "Do not take revenge, my friends, but leave room for God's wrath, for it is written: 'It is mine to avenge; I will repay,' says the Lord." Revenge is God's business, not yours, so try hard to keep yourself under control.

Talk to someone. Sometimes it helps to put your feelings into words. By letting somebody know you're angry, it can actually make you feel less angry. Try these helpful sayings: "I'm as angry as a mad scientist." "I'm furious like an F-5 tornado." "I'm as irritated as an itchy wool sweater." "I'm fuming like some really bad perfume."

Cool down. Get away from the situation—or person—that's making you angry by taking a walk, reading a book, or counting to 100. The Bible says Christ followers should work on their self-control. Proverbs 29:11 (NIrV) puts it this way: "A foolish person lets his anger run wild. But a wise person keeps himself under control." Do you want to be known as foolish or wise? It's best to choose now, before anger chooses for you.

Forgive. Of all the great things God gives you, forgiveness may be the most important. He forgives all the bad stuff you do. You're perfect and blameless in God's eyes. When you get angry, you not only should ask God to forgive your thoughts and actions, but you also should ask Him to help you forgive the person who wronged you. Like Jesus said, "When you stand praying, forgive anyone you have anything against. Then your Father in heaven will forgive your sins" (Mark 11:25, NIrv). If you don't forgive, it's easy to become bitter at the other person and for your anger never to go away.

GOD'S GUIDE

Read: Matthew 5:21-24

- Why do you think Jesus compares murder with being angry at someone? How are these two things the same?
- Does Jesus think it's important for you to ask forgiveness from people you've wronged? How can you tell?

_____

_____

_____

BONUS ACTIVITY

Create an "anger jar." Every time you get angry, write down why you're mad and who you're mad at. Then drop the note into the jar. Remember that God forgives you just as He wants you to forgive others. As the jar fills up (hopefully this will take a long time), focus on forgiving others and thank God for always forgiving you.

11

My youth group is so cool. Every summer we can sign up for "Peak Performance"—a weekend hiking trip that goes way up in the mountains of Colorado, which I think is near Denver.

I'm not really good at geometry, so I don't know where the city of Colorado is. I do know, however, that I'm finally old enough to go with my youth group on this awesome adventure. We're all very excited. In fact, my youth leader has been praying about me going with them for months now!

My youth pastor is great. He constantly for-gives me for little things that happen. For instance, three weeks ago we were talking about materialism (which I learned meant "loving our stuff too much"). We were supposed to bring something we owned that we really loved. I brought my two goldfish, Goldy and Nemo.

It would've been fine had my family not been super late to church or had I seen the bags of food for the needy on the floor in the lobby. I was in full sprint when I tripped over the bags. Goldy and Nemo flew out of my fishbowl and landed safely in our lost-and-found box. The fishbowl didn't do as well—it smashed into a million pieces.

I knew I had to clean up the mess before all the classes let out and church began, but I also had to quickly get my fish in some water. I frantically dug through the lost-and-found box, saved my two fish, and discovered my jacket, my sunglasses, my water gun, one of my shoes, and a half-eaten sucker that I had left in the bathroom several months before. It was red but tasted like butterscotch. I didn't know where to take my fish until I looked in the sanctuary and saw the baptistery (which I learned is where people are baptized). *Perfect!*

After dropping Goldy and Nemo into their new supersized, temporary fish bowl, I cleaned up the glass and water. It took so long that I missed Sunday school class. I followed the rest of my youth group into the church auditorium.

The sermon was really good that day. But the highlight was that a kid named Randy, who'd been studying the Bible for months, decided to be baptized! I was really excited for him until he got in the baptistery.

"Randy has decided to be baptized today to follow Jesus' example and to dec—" the preacher was saying when Randy interrupted with a scream: "AAAAUUUUGGGHHHHHHH!!!!!"

I'm not sure, but I think that was the point when I remembered my fish. Randy jumped out of the water, which scared the preacher too. I quickly leaped into action, screaming, "It's okay. They won't bite!"

Looking back, I probably could have explained myself better. Our preacher jumped out of the water and into Randy's arms. I ran over and caught Goldy but had a little trouble finding Nemo.

I thought Randy and my youth group would be mad at me for ruining such a great moment. However, they were very cool about it. Randy even said that I made it more memorable.

My youth group is like a built-in set of friends ready to encourage and help out. Here's a perfect example. I was having trouble getting my four bags in the baggage compartment under the bus we were taking to Peak Performance. Big Tim, a kid in the youth group, came over and loaded everything, then shut the door.

I had to bang on the door so someone would let me out of the baggage compartment. Apparently I looked like a suitcase, or Big Tim just got carried away helping me out!

A youth group is guys and girls who believe the same thing you believe and will eventually end up in the same place as you—heaven! Only at that

Did You Know?

- Kids who attend church enjoy life more and tend to get in less trouble.
- About half of all tweens in the United States attend a church service every weekend.
- Tweens who attend church six or more times per week often grow beards and start looking more like Jesus' disciples—and that's just the girls.
- Christianity is the world's largest religion with two billion believers.
  Note: One of these statistics breaks the bounds of believability, so don't believe it!

time we'll all have supernatural bodies, so walking up a mountain won't be any trouble at all, even those gargantuan Kansas mountains that my dad has been telling me about.

Super Average Advice

Youth groups can be a lot of fun. Gross food contests, scavenger hunts, silly games, small-group discussions, and inspiring messages from the Bible bring kids closer together and closer to God.

But maybe your youth group or Sunday school class isn't so fun. Somebody once said, "The only problem with Christianity is the Christians." Christians aren't perfect; we just follow a perfect Savior. Youth groups are made up of imperfect people, so there can still be cliques, backbiting, and a lot of drama. Maybe this scene sounds familiar:

Amanda: Jenny, I can't believe you're wearing that! T-shirts are so last week. All the cool Christians only wear jackets. I'm not your friend anymore.

Jenny: (starting to cry) I didn't know. *Waaaaaa!*

That may be a little exaggerated, but sometimes going to church can be hurtful. Sometimes it can be boring. But the fact remains that as a follower of Christ, it's important to get together with other kids who believe the same things you do.

Attending church and youth group is key because:

It shows you love God. You should try to worship and grow closer to God every day by reading the Bible and praying. But when God gave the Ten Commandments to the children of Israel, one of the commandments stated that one day of the week should be a day of rest to remember who God is and what He's done (Deuteronomy 5:12-15). Later in the book of Deuteronomy it says, "Love the LORD your God and keep his requirements, his decrees, his laws and his commands always" (11:1). You show God that you love Him when you follow what He wants you to do. And He wants people to be part of a body of believers.

It gives you the opportunity to encourage others and be encouraged. People are stronger when they work together. It's true in school, sports, chores, and church. The message in Hebrews 10:24-25 is clear: "And let us consider how we may spur one another on toward love and good deeds. Let us not give up meeting together, as some are in the habit of doing, but let us encourage one another." It's easier to stand up for God when you're standing shoulder to shoulder with a friend. A confidence comes in knowing you're not alone in your belief and devotion to God.

God's Guide

Read: Ephesians 4:11-16

- How do you see yourself serving God: telling others about Him, helping others, teaching others about Him?

- Think about how it feels when your leg or arm falls asleep. Does your body work well when part of it is sleeping? Do you think the same thing is true in the body of Christ? Are you doing your job or are you asleep? What can you do to wake up other parts of Christ's body?

_____

_____

_____

_____

Bonus Question

Can you name all 46 state capitals?

12

"These mosquitoes are horrible, and it's too hot here!" I shouted.

"Well, shut your window and let the bus air conditioning do its job," my youth pastor said. "We'll be leaving for our Peak Performance trip in about five minutes."

I was finally going with my youth group to climb a big mountain in Colorado! Of course, you can't just go climb a mountain without training. You have to prepare your body for it. So I've been getting in shape for a little over three whole days!

The first thing I did to get in mountain-climbing

shape was run up the stairs at school, instead of using the handicap ramp. I'm told that I didn't pass out that long. I got pretty winded the second day, but you can't just all of a sudden leap up six steps without a little heavy breathing. The next day, I did the stairs without any problem at all! Of course, this disappointed the crowd that had gathered to watch. However, it confirmed in my mind that I was ready for the mountain—well, almost ready.

I also started carrying extra weight with me as I walked around school. I knew I'd have to carry my food and sleeping bag up the mountain, so I started walking around school with a jar of pickles and my . . . uh . . . I mean, my little brother's stuffed teddy bear. Sure, I got some strange looks, but I was in training. I trained this way for only two days because I felt my body adapted pretty quick to the extra weight. Plus, Pat ate my pickles during math class, and I kept leaving behind my . . . uh . . . my little brother's teddy bear.

My youth group arrived at the base of Mount of the Holy Cross—yes, that's the real name— around noon. Driving there was pretty boring until we got into the mountains.

Now I don't know if you've ever seen a mountain, but the ones in Colorado are gynormous! The top of Mount of the Holy Cross is over 14,000 feet high, which is about a mile from the sun. We had only two days to climb, so we headed out quickly.

Our youth leader told us to bring plenty of water and protein. I knew that water was one of the ingredients in Coke, so I brought plenty of "water" with me. And Snickers bars are packed with protein! I thought I was all set.

However, I didn't realize that we'd be trekking up and down trails all day. At one point, I fell and all but two of my Coke cans exploded in my backpack. It was so sticky and covered with dirt, grass, and pine needles that I blended into the environment. I know people who've paid lots of money for a camouflage backpack—now I had one for free! (I always look for the positive in any situation.)

Plus, my pack was much lighter. This was good because evidently scientists take 90 percent of the oxygen out of the mountain air to use down in the cities. Breathing in the high country is very difficult. I was able to do it only once every two or three minutes.

Another strange thing I noticed is that things felt heavier the higher we got up the mountain—especially my sleeping bag, which I always thought was made out of light, fluffy cotton. But I guess it's actually lined with small rocks and part of an anvil.

We hiked all day for about 47 hours straight. I felt very weak and out of shape despite the fact that I'd eaten three Snickers. We finally stopped for dinner. I took out my frozen pizza only to realize that no one had brought a microwave. Talk about not planning ahead! My youth leader gave me a long talk about eating the proper food. He then gave me a bunch of raw vegetables, a bottled water, and a protein bar. I couldn't believe how much better I felt. I had enough energy to walk for another 10 minutes!

Later that night as I laid my sleeping bag on a

bed of rocks and grabbed my . . . uh . . . my little brother's stuffed teddy bear, I realized something. If you want to do your best, you have to be in your best shape.

The Bible tells us to put on the full armor of God, but it doesn't do us much good if our health prevents us from fighting the good fight. We have to take care of our bodies both inside and out! Eating naturally colorful foods (such as spinach, salad, or ketchup—not Nerds and M&M's) and chowing on plenty of protein makes a person strong. I suggest sardines, if you don't mind sleeping outside for four days until the smell goes away. And get plenty of exercise—six push-ups and four stairs are a good start.

Take care of your body so you are constantly ready for the battle or the big climb. Now if you will excuse me, I think I'll have another candy bar—that is, if I can ever find where I laid my backpack.

Super Average Advice

Your body is an amazing God-created machine. Depending on how you take care of it and what kind of fuel you put inside, you can have a high-powered, turbo-charged Corvette or a broken-down wagon with three wheels.

God created everybody with unique talents,

abilities, and body types, so you might notice that it's easier for some kids to build muscles, shoot a basketball, or play the piano. Some tweens may be able to eat an entire buffet without gaining an ounce, while others have to be more careful with their diet and exercise. But there are a few principles that can help everybody get the full potential out of their bodies.

Food. You are what you eat—literally. (That can be pretty scary if you're consuming a lot of turkey.) If you're eating junk food, you'll feel junky. The healthier you eat, the better you'll feel.

The food guide pyramid states that whole grains, vegetables, fruits, milk and calcium-rich foods, and meat, beans, fish, and nuts are key to a good diet. It's best to avoid soda, candy bars, and potato chips. Read Daniel 1:8-15 for a cool story about eating your veggies!

Exercise. Running, jumping, biking, swimming. The words are fun to say (try it), and the activities are great for your body. Anything that gets you moving, from full-contact karaoke to speed golf, helps build muscles and bones. In fact, the more exercise you do now, the healthier your bones will be when you're older. You don't have to play a team sport to get exercise. Sit-ups, push-ups, mowing the lawn, and walking the dog can be fun ways to keep your body fit.

Sleep. Did you know that not getting enough sleep can cause you to gain weight? Weird, huh. God designed your body to get a little over nine hours of sleep per night. When you don't sleep enough, you can get the munchies and crave junk foods. A lack of sleep also makes it harder for you to concentrate in school and can cause you to get cranky. Sleep gives your body time to rebuild muscles and reenergize your brain. Plus, it's easy to do. Just lie still and close your eyes.

God's Guide

Read: 1 Corinthians 6:19
- Think about what it truly means that your body is no longer yours, but God's.
- Write down ways that you can treat your body like a temple. Here are two ideas to get you started: never smoking cigarettes, drinking more water . . .

_____

_____

_____

_____

Vegetarians say that you should never eat red meat. That's true. Always eat brown meat!

BACKSTABBING BUDDY

13

It's very hard to know who to trust, trust me!

Once I trusted this guy at the mall. He said if I bought this new shirt, every girl at school would think I was cool.

I learned a great lesson because of that shirt. You can't trust girls to deal honestly with their emotions. I bought the shirt and every girl I saw fought her desire to talk to me. In fact, most of them walked away quickly. I wore that shirt for six days in a row hoping to find some girl that could be trusted to face her own feelings. But every day every girl stayed farther and farther away.

I also trusted Donny once when he said he could knock a milk carton off my head with a rubber band. Looking back, I kind of wish I had used an empty milk carton. I set the chocolate milk on my head. Donny pulled back the rubber band on his finger and let it fly. He hit me in the neck! He wasn't even close to the carton.

Of course, he pointed out that the milk carton did fall off my head. I wanted to argue with him, but I couldn't talk at the moment. Plus, I couldn't see because of the milk running through my hair and into my eyes.

It's just hard to know who to trust.

Sometimes my youth group plays the "trust fall" game. They pick a kid from the group who hopefully hasn't recently consumed a lot of liquids. This kid climbs on top of a chair or a table or a four-story window. He then turns his back toward the crowd and falls backward without looking, hoping his friends will catch him, therefore proving that he trusts them. But sometimes it doesn't work. Sometimes a trust fall can quickly resemble a bad fall if you don't have the right friends.

The first time I did the trust fall, four kids in my youth group volunteered to catch me. These were four kids that I didn't really trust. They weren't the regular kids who attended youth group;

they usually showed up only if we were doing something fun involving food or video games. If we were playing a video game that required us to eat a lot of food, they were definitely there!

I had my doubts that they would catch me. But I put my faith in them anyway, and fell back from the table. I didn't remember the table being 40 feet tall when I climbed up there. You would think I would have noticed something like that. However, I did notice it as I fell backwards through the air for about 20 minutes. In fact, the fall was so long that several times I actually had to stop screaming and take another breath of air. It went something like this:

"Aaaauuuuggghhhhhhhhhhhhh (gulp of air) *Auuuuugggghhhhhhh!* (another gulp of air) *AuuggghhhOhMyWhenWillThisFallEndAuugggghhhhh* (stop to look at my watch) *Auuuggghhhhhhhhhhhhhh* (pull out my dad's BlackBerry and check my e-mail) *Auuuugggghhhhhhhhhh!* Oh, they caught me!"

I had great faith in these kids—until I opened my eyes. Standing on each side of me was my youth leader and a regular youth group kid named Randy. The kids who were supposed to catch me had stepped back, thinking it would be funny to let me fall. Randy and my youth leader quickly jumped in and saved me.

"I can't believe you caught me!" I shouted with joy.

"Well, you weigh only about 20 pounds," Randy said. "You just floated down, which gave us time to step in."

"Yeah," my youth leader added. "And next time, please don't drink so many liquids before you come to youth group."

We have to pick our friends carefully. Some kids pretend to be your friend but will stab you in the back the second you aren't looking. This world is out of control, even with superheroes like you and me in it. Satan is here, and that means evil exists. The guy who invented the time-out is just

Did You Know?

- Backstabbing was one of the first events in the early Greek Olympics.*
- Almost everybody will be stabbed in the back by a friend during their tween years.
- Seeking revenge is not the best way to handle a backstabbing friend.
* They called it javelin throwing back then.

one example of evil.

But even when our friends turn away from us or nasty rumors circulate about us, remember that Jesus will be there. He's a true friend who will never leave and will never stab us in the back.

And the cool thing is, when we fall into His arms at the end of our lives, He will take us up to heaven where we will never fall again! I can't wait, because halfway up to heaven we should all be able to see the top of that table I fell off of!

Until then, we should pick our friends based on how closely they resemble Jesus. Otherwise, they will probably just stab us in the back or let us down.

Now if you will excuse me, Billy has a milk carton on his head, so I have to see how well I can shoot a rubber band.

Super Average Advice

Nothing causes more pain than when a friend stabs you in the back, except maybe eating a whole jalapeño pepper and chugging a bottle of Tabasco sauce. That can *really* bring a tear to your eye! But seriously, it hurts when a trusted friend turns against you. Your feelings can include:

- betrayal
- confusion
- euphoria—*not really*

- anger
- wanting revenge
- sadness

A lot of times it'd probably feel better for your friend to punch you in the stomach rather than stab you in the back. At least you could see the punch coming. And that's what hurts the most about back-stabbing friends—often you didn't realize anything was wrong.

King David went through a lot of tough situations described in the Bible. He battled a giant, killed a lion, had his boss throw a spear at him, and, worst of all, was stabbed in the back by a friend. Psalm 41:9 says, "Even my close friend, whom I trusted, he who shared my bread, has lifted up his heel against me."

While there's probably no way you can avoid being stabbed in the back, you can make a plan to deal with it when it happens.

Talk to your friend. Even though it may be difficult, ask your friend why she stabbed you in the back. Try to stay calm and explain how you feel. The Bible gives some good advice in Proverbs 15:1 (NIrV): "A gentle answer turns anger away. But mean words stir up anger." If you lash out at your friend, it'll only cause more trouble. By staying in control of your emotions, you may be able to figure out why your friend stabbed you in the back and restore the relationship (or decide you don't want her as a friend anymore).

Forgive your friend. True forgiveness isn't easy, but it is important. Ephesians 4:31-32 says, "Get rid of all bitterness, rage and anger, brawling and slander, along with every form of malice. Be kind and compassionate to one another, forgiving each other, just as in Christ God forgave you." If you stay angry at a backstabbing friend, it hurts you more than it hurts your friend. Don't become bitter. Let your friend know that you forgive her for her actions. Your forgiveness may help your friend realize that she made a mistake and lost a good friend.

BONUS ACTIVITY

You can practice being the catcher for a trust fall using your cat. If it won't voluntarily fall backwards off a table, you can just toss him up and down in the air for a while. Just be sure to have some Band-Aids nearby!

God's Guide

Read: Matthew 26:47-50

- Jesus was stabbed in the back by one of His closest friends. (Of course, being God, Jesus knew it was coming.) Put yourself in Jesus' shoes. What was He probably thinking when Judas kissed Him?
- Does it help you deal with backstabbing friends knowing that Jesus went through the same thing?
- What response should you have when a friend stabs you in the back?

_____

_____

_____

_____

_____

_____

EXXXCCCUUUSSSSEEEE ME!

14

BUUUURRRRRPPPPPPP!

"What do you say when you burp at the table?" my mom snapped.

"Sorry," Grandmother replied. "Excuse me."

Everyone has his or her own idea of the proper way to act in front of other people. Grown-ups call it etiquette. I don't even want to try pronouncing that word, so I call it manners.

Some think it's bad manners not to place your napkin in your lap. Others think good manners consist of wiping your mouth on the tablecloth, instead of your shirtsleeve. Some people say "Yes, ma'am," when a lady asks a question. Others think it's okay to nod or grunt a reply—just as long as they *don't* say, "You got it, Chick."

My parents are really big on good manners. They've stressed the importance of saying "please" and "thank you," so I always try to throw in those words. Here are some examples:

• "Please let me explain why the cat is covered with moss."

• "Thank you for not grounding me for a month; I didn't know the cat didn't like to swim."

Yup, there's nothing as important as using the "magic" words: *please, thank you,* and *look out for that crazed cat!* (I recently added the last one, and it has proved to be very helpful.)

My family not only believes in acting your best, but also in looking your best. This starts early in the morning. Mom says taking a shower is important. I agree with her, sort of. I usually play in the creek behind our house and that keeps me clean. Besides, grown-ups pay a lot of money for mud masks and moss body wraps. I get both every day for free! My mom also has problems with my hair. She thinks it usually looks like a bird's nest. I disagree. I think that birds keep landing on me because they like me.

Sometimes on special occasions, Mom insists

on styling my hair with a brush that must be made out of barbed wire and broken glass. Not only does this rip into my scalp and make my hair lay down, it also opens up my vocal cords. I have a beautiful screaming—I mean, singing—voice in the morning. She then gives me a speech about being polite and minding my manners throughout the day.

I usually say, "You got it, Chick!" Sometimes she laughs. Sometimes she just combs my hair again. But, as always, I know my parents are right about manners. I've found that when I'm polite, adults treat me better. The first time I realized this was last year.

Did You Know?

- When someone asks you to pass the salt, it's proper etiquette to pass the salt *and* the pepper.
- You can make a good first impression by firmly shaking an adult's hand and looking him or her directly in the eye.
- It's proper manners only for grandmas to greet you by pinching your cheeks and saying, "Aren't you cute?" If your cousin tries it, you can tackle him.

My teacher, Mrs. Hines, said it was very dangerous to lean back in our chairs. She had a strict No-Leaning-Back-in-Your-Chair policy in her class. Knowing this rule, I was very careful when I leaned back in my chair. Usually, I did it when she wasn't looking. One day I leaned way back in my chair with my head hanging upside down. I was trying to get my nose parallel to the floor so Zander could try to toss a Skittles into one of my nostrils. I should point out that it was science class, and we were testing a theory.

Well, I leaned way past the safe point, but I did get my nostrils perfectly pointed upward as Zander tossed a red Skittles toward my nose. Here's what I don't understand. How could the quarterback of our football team be so bad at throwing Skittles? The candy hit me right in the eye, and I went crashing to the floor! I remember thinking two things:

1. Mrs. Hines was totally right about the danger of leaning back in your chair.

2. Someone had stuck gum on the ceiling.

Mrs. Hines came running to the back of the room.

"Mr. Smiley!" she yelled.

"Yes, ma'am?" I said, trying to sit up. (Note: It's never good when a teacher calls you by your last name.)

"What's the rule about chairs?" she asked.

"Pick one based on comfort and whether it matches your kitchen table," I said, hoping to lighten the mood.

She then began a long lecture about her chair rule. I kept saying, "Yes, ma'am," "I'm sorry, ma'am," and "No, ma'am, I'm not on any medication."

At the end of her speech, she paused.

"Look," she said, "I can tell you're a nice boy with good manners, so I'm not going to send you to detention. Just be careful, and follow the rules from now on."

Of course, God doesn't want us to have good manners just to escape getting into trouble. That's just a bonus He threw in! He wants us to always act our best in front of people. Being rude will not only keep us from making friends, it will also hurt our chances of telling some people about God.

Now if you will excuse me, I'm in the mood for some gum. I need a ladder. *Where is that janitor?*

Super Average Advice

When it comes to good manners, it seems like there's a rule for everything:

- Hold open the door for women.
- Always say "please," "thank you," and "excuse me."

- Don't shout in the library.
- Set the table with the napkin on the left side of the plate.
- Never play a trumpet in a moving car.
- Look at people when they're talking.
- Don't rest your elbows on the table.
- Burping the ABCs may be impressive, but it's not socially acceptable.
- Greet relatives you haven't seen in a while with a hug and a "hello."
- Never roll your eyes.
- Bow your head and close your eyes when you say grace.
- Call adults Mr., Mrs., Ms., or Miss and his or her last name.
- Avoid yanking a dog's tail.

There are lots of other rules. In fact, there are so many rules that it may seem impossible to have good manners. So instead of trying to memorize a bunch of rules, it's best to focus on the reasons behind the rules.

You become more attractive. No, your zits won't suddenly disappear and your hair won't mysteriously start flowing stunningly in the wind. But people will want to hang out with you. Nobody wants to be friends with someone who's rude and mean. Good manners get you noticed and draw friends to you.

You show other people respect. The Bible is big on respect. When Jesus walked the earth, He showed respect to the lowest people in society—the sick and the outcast. He touched people that others would never touch. He came to serve. He was completely unselfish. Romans 15:2 (NIrv) says, "We should all please our neighbors. Let us do what is good for them. Let us build them up." You can please your neighbors by having good manners. When you use proper etiquette (don't worry, I still can't pronounce it either), you build up the people around you.

You put your faith in action. Not only can your good manners make others feel good, but you can actually show Christ's love with your actions. When you hold open the door for a mom carrying a baby or let an older person move ahead of you in a line at the store, you're displaying God's love. The Bible says Christians stand out by the love they show. If you have the opportunity to help someone or show good manners, remember this verse: "My little children, let us not love in word or in tongue, but in deed and in truth" (1 John 3:18, NKJV). That means don't just talk about having good manners or memorize a list of rules; get out there and let God's light shine through your actions. God may use your good manners to encourage somebody to start a relationship with Him.

God's Guide

Read: Philippians 2:3-4

- What do these verses have to do with good manners?
- How is being selfish the opposite of having good manners?
- When you humble yourself and think of other people as more important, how does that make you treat them?

_____

_____

_____

Bonus Activity

See how many Skittles you can throw in the air and catch in your mouth at one time. Then use good manners by cleaning up after yourself. The ones that hit the floor can always be given to your brother or sister!

15

I should've known better than to try to finish my math homework on the school bus. Our bus was superbouncy. It was so bouncy that Donny's football kept flying out of his hands and hitting me on the head. How it bounced from four rows behind and hit me every time is an equation I hope doesn't show up on my math homework.

I finally started watching for it. The next time it flew at me—I ducked. This worked for me, but didn't turn out too well for Glasses McQueen, a seventh-grader with really big, round glasses. As the football hit him in the throat, Glasses let out a mighty "Whoooooooooooooo!" sound.

I didn't mean to laugh, but Glasses' glasses already made him look like an owl. Now he sounded like one, too. I catapulted over the seat—our bumpy bus made it easy to do—and landed next to Glasses.

"You okay?" I asked.

"Yeah," he said. "But can you help me find my glasses?"

"That's easy," I said. "They're huge!"

Glasses McQueen's glasses are famous around school. McQueen says they have superpowers. On a sunny day, he can actually burn things just by looking at them! He let me take a peek through them once. It was like looking into a fun house mirror. Everything appeared all blurry and wavy. People had tiny legs, eight-foot-long stomachs, and huge heads shaped like traffic cones.

Glasses told me that was another one of the glasses' superpowers. If anyone except him looked through them, the glasses would mess up his vision on purpose. I wore them for about 10 minutes and I couldn't see a thing the entire time.

I tried to wear them to history class. As I walked down the hall with my hands out like a zombie, I turned into a room that I *thought* was my history class. The room was completely quiet.

"Anyone in here?" I shouted.

"Shhhhhhhh!" came a voice I didn't recognize.

"Oh, I get it," I said, walking toward a blurry person who was either sitting behind a desk or on a furry rock. "You want me to guess who you are."

I reached out my hand and grabbed the person's face.

"I know you," I said. "You're a traffic cone!"

That's when a purse hit me.

"This is the gifted class, and we're taking a test!" the traffic cone shouted. "You aren't supposed to be in here."

The rest of the cone-headed blurry monsters started throwing things at me. Realizing my mistake, I turned and tried to find the door. I started feeling my way along the wall, but I was being pelted with lots of pencils, pocket protectors, and one big calculator.

"I can't see!" I finally said, "Someone get me out of here."

Gifted kids are supposed to be good listeners, but I don't think they heard me right. In fact, several of them must have heard, "Throw more stuff at me."

Fortunately, the teacher jumped to my rescue.

"Take off the glasses!" she said. "You're about to step on my calculator." I took off the superpower glasses, apologized, and ran to find McQueen.

Anyway, back on the bus, I reached down and found the glasses on the floor. Glasses put them on and smiled.

"That was a cool thing to do, Jerry," a voice said from behind me. It was Clint. I knew it was Clint, not because I saw him but because I could smell his leather jacket.

"I'm still going by 'Bob' but only because that's my name," I answered. "And thanks."

"Here," Clint said, reaching into his back-pack and pulling out a CD. "I burned this yesterday. It's cool."

I already knew it'd be cool, because Clint was so cool. I took the CD home and played it. I couldn't

Did You Know?

- Fifty percent of music fans said they've made free copies of downloaded music.
- iPod stands for "I play only downloads."*
- One student at the University of Arizona had a computer with more than $50 million worth of pirated music and movies on it.

* Not really, but it *should* stand for that.

really tell if it was Christian music or not. At one point after the singer had evidently shot somebody and punched another guy, he did say God's name. I'm supposed to listen only to Christian music, but I figured this was okay because it did have God's name in it. Plus, I wasn't really listening to the words. I just loved the beat, so I listened to it non-stop for a week.

On Friday, I was up in my room, blasting out the new CD in my headphones. No one was around, so I loudly sang the words. About 10 minutes into the music, I turned around and saw my great-grandparents standing in my bedroom doorway. At first I thought they wanted to show me their new dentures, because their mouths were wide open. I soon found out they were shocked at what I was singing.

"What did I say?" I asked, embarrassed.

I skipped back and listened carefully to the song. Now it was my turn to show the inside of my mouth. I hadn't noticed the lyrics. All week I'd just been listening to the music, and I guess my fantastical brain memorized the words without me even knowing it. (Hey, maybe I *should* be in the gifted class.)

That day I learned I have to be careful what I listen to because my brain picks up on it. (I also found out my great-grandparents have really white teeth!) I guess that's why my parents want me to listen to Christian music—to put good stuff in my brain, not for the white teeth.

Anyway, I apologized to my great-grandparents. I told them the whole story. My great-grandfather was especially interested in trying on those super-power glasses. I hope he knows what he's doing. Those things are dangerous.

Super Average Advice

Not everything that's played on the radio will be music to your ears. A ton of popular tunes contain language and talk about things that would:

- make a professional wrestler blush and squirm uncomfortably;
- cause your grandparents to have a heart attack;
- force your parents to scream, "Turn off that junk!";
- hurt your walk with Christ and your witness to others.

Just because a song has a cool beat and all your friends listen to it doesn't make it okay for your iPod. As a follower of Christ, you're called to a higher standard. Your iPod is a reflection of you. Allow only good stuff in.

Different is good. Sometimes your faith in Christ will make you feel like an outsider compared to your friends. They may listen to the latest hits, wear the most current fashions, and watch blockbuster music videos. Your family may decide to avoid those things. As it says in Romans 12:2, "Do not conform any longer to the pattern of this world, but be transformed by the renewing of your mind." Choosing not to follow the crowd is a good thing when it protects your mind and keeps you focused on Christ.

Music is good. Not all music should be chucked in the trash. You just need to make the right choice when you put on your headphones. The Bible talks a lot about music. King David was a gifted musician. He wrote, "Lord, it is good to praise you. Most High God, it is good to make music to honor you" (Psalm 92:1, NIrV).

Be honest with yourself as you listen to music. Ask yourself how it makes you feel. Does it make you feel happy? Depressed? Excited? Anxious? Closer to God? Songs can have a powerful impact on you. Try hard to ensure that impact is a positive one.

Following the law is good. This one sounds like a no-brainer, right? Wrong. Millions of songs are *stolen* every year. It's estimated that 10 million people share music files each day. According to United States Copyright Law, that's stealing. When you buy a CD or pay to download a tune from the Internet, it gives you the right to listen to it. It *doesn't* allow you to burn a copy for a friend or let a buddy rip it to his MP3 player.

The law states that each song has a value between $750 and $30,000 (although most people don't have to pay fines that large if they're caught). But that means a few pirated songs can add up to a big problem. So follow the law and pay for the music you listen to.

God's Guide

Read: 1 Thessalonians 5:21-24
- Think of ways you can "test" the music you hear to make sure it is good.
- Why do you think God wants you to keep your spirit, soul, and body healthy and blameless?
- How does listening to bad music harm your spirit, soul, and body?

_____

_____

_____

Tie a blindfold over your eyes and see if you can identify different family members by feeling their faces. (Note: Don't confuse your great-grandmother with your dog. Trust me, both will be mad at you!)

16

"Bob, do you have your shoes on?" my dad asked.

Uh-oh!

My brother and I have figured out that we don't have to do as many spontaneous chores if we don't have our shoes on. This causes us to take our shoes off the instant we get near our house. I once even got off the school bus with my shoes in my hand just in case my dad was waiting by the door! But sometimes I forget.

Dad'll come in the living room and say, "Bob, do you have your shoes on?" I sadly say, "Uh . . .

yes." He then says, "Great! Could you go out and sweep the highway that runs into town?" or something like that.

I recently looked up the word *chore* in the dictionary. Okay, I had my brother look it up, but he owed me a favor because I finally put the ladder back up so he could get down out of the tree. But that's another story. The definition of *chore* reads, "A difficult or disagreeable task." My dad defines the term differently. He says chores help parents and contribute to the family. That must be the King James Version.

One time Dad tried to motivate me to do my chores by saying, "When Abe Lincoln was your age, he had four jobs!" I then pointed out that when Abe Lincoln was *his* age, he was the president of the United States.

Okay, that's really not true. Actually, Lincoln was serving in the Illinois legislature. (I guess my dad's love of history got passed down a generation.) But I knew Dad was right, so I took his advice and tried to work hard.

The first thing I did was mow our lawn. However, Dad thought I should mow our *entire* yard in one day! I wanted to keep things simple: Mow a strip or two of grass; drink some lemonade; watch some TV; celebrate my birthday and Christmas; and then mow another strip or two. This seemed like a good pace for me. After all, I didn't want to overdo it.

I came up with another idea that my mom didn't like—mowing after dark. It just doesn't cool down enough to be outside until after midnight. And in my defense, I did offer her free earplugs and remind her that the flowers—and bushes—would eventually grow back.

Since I started doing chores, I've learned some important lessons.

No. 1. If you see a snake, look closely before attacking it. I was pulling some weeds when I thought I saw a snake by our fence. I grabbed a rake and chopped it to pieces! My dad instantly ran outside. I assumed it was to thank me for my heroic snake-killing skills, but he just said, "Do you know why the cable TV just went out?"

No. 2. Be careful about the sun. During an extremely hot day, I took off my shirt as I helped my mom replant some flowers. Now I know why it's called a flower bed, because somehow I drifted off to sleep. When I woke up, I could hear bacon sizzling. Then I realized the sound was coming from my back! Dad tried to heat up his TV dinner just by placing it on me. So the lesson is to always wear sunscreen and to stay away from flower beds unless you're hyped up on caffeine.

No. 3. Plates don't make good Frisbees. Okay,

the plastic ones work. But try not to throw your mom's good china. I learned this when my brother and I decided to help clear the table after a fancy dinner. I ran to the sink while my brother grabbed

Did You Know?

- During the heyday of mining, children went deep underground to push out the ore carts. This is how the word *chore* came about: **ch**i*ld* + **ore = chore.**
- Nine out of ten kids help out around the house.
- Kids do about 12 percent of all work performed around the house.
  Warning: Some mining stories may be make-believe.

plates off the table and started throwing them at me. I caught the first one all right. But the next one caught me in the forehead and knocked me over. The third plate sailed right through the kitchen and into the living room. Fortunately, very few plates broke—a fact my mom was happy to hear after she recovered from her fainting spell.

No. 4. Cats don't like baths. This lesson came

with lots of screeching, howling, scratching, Band-Aids, and Neosporin—and that was all for my dad. Maybe I should have waited to give the cat a bath until Dad was out of the tub. But now I understand cats don't like baths; cats prefer to take showers.

Anyway, don't forget to thank God for your family. Helping your family by doing chores is one way you can show them your love. And if you need part of your lawn mowed, give me a call. I could use a couple of bucks right now—I still owe my mom for two plates.

Super Average Advice

It's no coincidence that *chore* rhymes with *bore*. Vacuuming, cleaning the bathroom, putting away dishes, making the bed, and picking up after pets don't usually rate too high when kids are asked, "What's your favorite thing to do?"

But helping around the house is part of growing up. Can you imagine heading off to college or moving out of your house without knowing how to work a washing machine or make dinner? You'd probably win an award for being the skinniest and smelliest kid around. The truth is, work helps you succeed in life. So try these things to make your chores not such a chore.

Create a schedule. Get in the habit of doing your chores at the same time every week. Make a chart and then cross things off. This can help in a couple of ways.

First, you won't have to think about what you have to do—you'll just do it. It'll be a natural part of your week, just like eating or breathing or chasing your cat when you see it. You might even miss doing chores if you're on vacation. Just kidding.

Second, your parents won't have to remind you to do your chores. Many parents say they constantly nag their kids to do housework. That's not fun for anybody; nobody likes to be nagged. And the nagger doesn't enjoy repeating the same thing over and over and over and over again. Instead of waiting to be told to do your chores, jump up and do them without being asked.

Remember why you do chores. Something doesn't have to be fun for you to enjoy it. There's satisfaction in completing a difficult task. When God created Adam, He put him in the Garden of Eden to work (Genesis 2:15). You're designed to work, too. When you help around the house, you honor God and your parents. Romans 12:10-11 (NIrV) says, "Love each other deeply. Honor others more than yourselves. Never let the fire in your heart go out. Keep it alive. Serve the Lord."

When you do chores, you're physically showing your parents that you love them. You're also serving God by obeying what your mom or dad asks you to do. Plus, working hard can make you feel good. So when you do chores, everybody wins!

GOD'S GUIDE

Read: Proverbs 14:23
- Name some of the "profits" from doing chores. Who benefits?
- What would happen if you only talked about doing chores but never got around to doing them?
- Think of your chores. Come up with a plan to complete them every week.

_____

_____

_____

_____

BONUS ACTIVITY

Duct tape a flashlight to a batting helmet and you suddenly have a miner's hat—good for mowing in the dark or waking up your brother!

GRANDPARENTS: OLDIES BUT GOODIES

17

Some kids don't like to hang out with their grandparents.

They'll say, "I don't like to talk to my grandparents. They're old and their minds wander. They say strange things."

I don't understand that kind of thinking. That's the best time to talk to them because it's like channel surfing on TV. You never know what's going to be on!

Personally, I love hanging out with my grandparents. And they love me. My grandfather always plays little games with me. For instance, when I go over to visit him, I'll run up and knock on the door.

"Who is it?" my grandfather says.

"It's your grandson!" I shout, knowing what's coming next.

"We moved! I mean, they moved," my grandfather says, trying to make his voice sound like someone else.

Then we'll play hide-and-seek. Grandpa disappears almost as soon as I walk in the house. Later my grandmother and I will find him somewhere, like in the basement or at Wal-Mart. My grandparents are awesome.

My grandmother is fun because she can't hear very well. Everything she says is superloud. Plus, she says whatever pops into her mind.

"It's too cold in here!" she once yelled. "Ask that man to turn on the heat!"

"I will as soon as he's done leading us in prayer," I whispered back to her, hoping the preacher wasn't too interrupted.

Every summer I get to spend a week with my grandparents. We play these old, antique games. One game is called "checkers." Each player has a certain number of round chips—either red or black. We move our checkers around on the board, trying to jump over our opponent's checkers. If I jump one of Grandpa's checkers, I can take it off the board and keep it. We play this until I take almost all of his checkers. Then he knocks over the board and scatters the checkers everywhere. It's a fun game. I wish I had a video-game version of it.

I also love hanging out with my grandparents because they have the coolest stories. My grandfather once suggested I start writing down my own stories. "Why don't you take these five notebooks and write down all your adventures?" he said. "You can come out of your room when you have 100 chapters done."

At night, after watching three episodes of an old TV show called *Matlock,* we usually turn off the television, and I listen to them tell stories. One time I said, "Wow, Grandma! You had a lot of adventures as a kid. You should have written them down like I'm doing."

My grandpa jumped in and said, "That would've been impossible. Paper hadn't been invented yet. You know how hard it would've been for her to chisel all those stone tablets." Then he disappeared for a weeklong game of hide-and-seek.

My grandmother also has this antique thing called a "photo album." Believe it or not, hundreds of years ago in the 1960s and 1970s, people didn't have digital cameras. They had to take pictures with a camera that I'm guessing was made out of rocks and tree branches. All the pictures were put on something called "film." The film had to be dropped off at a special store. After that, people would go home and wait about a year. Finally, the store would call and let them know the pictures were ready to be picked up. All the pictures would be printed on thick pieces of small rectangular paper. What a crazy world they lived in!

Anyway, my grandmother has a book with all these pictures of people in it. I like the book because it has a picture of every person that my grandpar-

Did You Know?

- More than half of all grandparents see their grandchildren at least once every two or three months.
- Grandparents spend an average of $500 a year on their grandchildren.
- Grandparent spelled backward is *tnerapdnarg* (pronounced ne-rap-dnarg; the *t* is silent), which is the Greek word for "raises those with a hairy fist."*

* Isn't it fun to make up Greek words?

ents taught about Jesus Christ! It's a book of people who are now going to heaven because of my grandparents. They're the coolest.

Another reason I like my grandparents is because the Bible challenges us to seek wisdom. Well, I've found it! My grandparents have a lot to offer. If you spend time with your grandparents, you'll discover the same thing. If you're fortunate enough that your grandparents or great-grandparents are still alive, I challenge you to seek their wisdom. In other words, let them teach you wise, smart things.

Speaking of seeking, I know my grandpa is hiding around here somewhere. I'm going to find one of those Home Depot employees to help me look.

Super Average Advice

In the United States alone, there are around 90 million grandparents. If all these grandparents held hands, that would make a very long line at the Old Country Buffet.

All joking aside, grandparents and great-grandparents can make a great big difference in your life.

• They have the time to listen to you and play games.

• They often enjoy spoiling you with affection and gifts.

• They can tell you stories about your parents that you never knew.

• They can share what life was like growing up without iPods, color TV, cell phones, and computers.

• They can be your best cheerleaders, encouraging you in the good times and bad.

While it's true that sometimes grandparents can have more health problems and get confused more easily, they can also be a never-ending source of love. Of course, some kids don't like visiting their grandparents. Hearing the same stories over and over and not having all the latest gadgets is boring. But even if Grandma's house isn't a thrill-a-minute amusement park, the Bible has some specific advice on how you should treat your grandparents.

Respect. Leviticus 19:32 says, "Rise in the presence of the aged, show respect for the elderly and revere your God." The message is obvious: Older people should be treasured, not ignored. Grandparents love to serve their families and make them feel special, so do your best to help them out. Offer to get them a drink, do yard work, or help with the dishes when you visit. Show them respect by spending time with them, asking questions about their lives, and listening to the answers. If you don't know your grandparents well, you may be surprised how cool they are.

Honor. You might think honor is similar to respect. You honor your grandparents when you follow the advice and wisdom that they share with you. Don't discard what they say just because they're from a different generation. Proverbs 20:29 (NIrV) says, "Young men are proud of their strength. Gray hair brings honor to old men."

Your grandparents may not be able to bench-press 400 pounds, but they can help you through a lot if you let them. And when they help you in some way—advice, a gift, money for college, an extra piece of dessert, a car—don't forget to say thank you.

Bonus Activity

Have a "strange story" contest with your grandparents. Each of you can tell two personal stories. The one with the strangest story wins.

GOD'S GUIDE

Read: 1 Peter 5:5-6

- What does it mean for younger people to submit to older folks?
- How can you show humility to your grandparents? Why is it important to be humble?

_____

_____

_____

_____

_____

_____

_____

18

I'm always about to do something really important when my mom asks me, "Have you done your homework?"

For instance, today I was working on an experiment. A kid in class said it takes 45 seconds for a Twinkie to explode in a microwave. To test this theory, as soon as I got home I unwrapped a Twinkie, put it in the microwave, and set the timer. Right before I hit the button, my mom walked into the kitchen. "Have you done your homework?"

No wonder scientists don't come up with anything cool anymore. Their moms probably keep stopping them right before a major breakthrough. "I think I can cure the common cold if I just add one more ingredient to my—*Ugh*, what is it, Mother? Fine, I'll go do my homework."

That must happen all the time.

Anyway, I went into my room and opened my homework folder. First, I had to read a short story. I love to read, so I dove right in. About halfway through the story some loud screaming interrupted me. Looking back, I guess I should've taken the Twinkie out of the microwave. Not only did I not get to see the Twinkie explode, but it ruined the cup of coffee my mom was heating up.

"Did you see how long it took to explode?" I asked, running into the kitchen.

Judging from the look Mom gave me, she doesn't care about science at all.

I went back, finished the story, and moved to math. I love math, except for the numbers. The first problem talked about a boy who had eight apples and needed $4 to buy something. I had to figure out how much the boy needed to charge for the apples in order to get four bucks.

This was so easy! I wrote down that the boy should mow one lawn and keep his apples. Most people pay at least $15 for lawn mowing. In fact, all the problems were like this, so I breezed through my math homework. I even wrote down some phone numbers of people who needed their lawns mowed.

With English and math complete, I only had to collect and identify six kinds of leaves for science. My mom has a whole book full of leaves that she has identified. I couldn't decide if that was cheating or not. The assignment didn't say where to get the leaves. It just said to get them.

An hour later Mom found me playing basketball in our driveway. I'm a really good jumper and can even dunk the ball if my dad parks his car in the right place. I was just leaping off the car when Mom said, "Have you finished your homework?"

I slammed the ball, hung on the rim, and started to tell her about my homework. But when my brother saw me, he thought I was a life-size piñata and ran at me with a Wiffle ball bat.

"Put down the bat," I yelled at Brian. "Mom, make him put down the bat. Here's some candy!"

I pulled some candy out of my pocket and threw it at my brother. However, I'm not strong enough to hold the rim with one hand and I came crashing to the ground.

"Well, have you finished your homework?" Mom asked again.

"I just studied gravity," I said, getting up.

We walked inside so I could show her my homework folder. Turns out my mom had completely different answers for my math homework. Then she got to my leaf collection.

"Bob, did you get all these leaves from around the house?"

"Yeah," I answered. "At first I was going to get them out of your leaf book. I knew it was wrong though, so I did it myself. It actually was kind of fun."

Mom looked at me and smiled. "I'm really proud of you for doing the right thing."

It was a great feeling . . . until she saw how I had identified them.

"I think your teacher wants the names of the leaves," she said, looking puzzled, "not for you to name the leaves."

"I call the big green one 'Spike'!" I said, grabbing the Wiffle ball bat.

"Where are you going?" she asked. "You need to identify these correctly."

"I will," I answered. "I just need to find my brother and get some candy to eat while I redo my math and science."

Super Average Advice

Nobody can doubt King Solomon's wisdom. So

maybe you agree with him when he said, "Much study wearies the body" (Ecclesiastes 12:12).

See, the Bible contains a lot of truth! School *can* drag you down. Reading about ancient wars, writing about summer vacation, and completing hundreds of math problems doesn't make most kids giddy with excitement. Just thinking about studying makes some students tired. Maybe you have a favorite subject in school. Working on assignments from your favorite class usually isn't a problem. The problem is that *every* class hands out homework.

A recent poll found that elementary students spend an average of 78 minutes per night on homework. During middle school, that number jumps up to 99 minutes. The average high schooler takes 105 minutes to finish nightly assignments. That's a lot of time to complete a pile of work.

In fact, many students say they were first tempted to cheat to save time and shave off minutes in completing their homework. But when students cheat, they cheat only themselves. Leviticus 19:11 says, "Do not steal. Do not lie. Do not deceive one another." When you cheat on a school assignment or test, you do all three:

- You *steal* a grade you didn't deserve.
- You *lie* about completing the work.
- You *deceive* your teacher into thinking you

know more about the subject than you actually do.

Despite all the problems caused by cheating, a lot of kids do it. Around 75 percent of high schoolers admit they cheated on a test. More and more kids copy assignments or research papers off the Internet. That's the problem.

Here's the solution according to the prophet Isaiah: "Learn to do right!" (Isaiah 1:17). Doing the right thing often means doing extra work. But God will bless your efforts. By working hard to complete homework and study for tests, you'll have the satisfaction of knowing you are doing your best— regardless of what grades you get. And while you're at it, try these homework tips:

1. Make a list of assignments. Many schools hand out planners so you can keep track of homework. Even if your school doesn't, compile a list of nightly assignments and upcoming projects. Not only will this help you stay organized, it also feels great to cross things off your list.

2. Create a place to study. Whether it's your bedroom, a home office, or the kitchen table, make sure you have a comfortable place to do homework that's bright, quiet, and well lit.

3. Finish homework before going on to fun activities. Sure, maybe you'll need a snack to calm your growling stomach or some time to wind down, but jump on your homework as soon as you can after school.

4. Ask a parent to help. Don't have your parents complete your homework for you (who knows what kind of grades they got in school?), but ask for pointers or have them check your answers when you're done.

By following a plan, you'll be able to take some of the "work" out of homework.

Did You Know?

- In a study that asked kids what they worry about most, 78 percent said "getting good grades."
- Cheating is okay because it doesn't hurt anybody.*
- Most often, students begin cheating when they start middle school because the homework requires more research and takes more time.

* Didn't you read the chapter?!? If you think cheating is okay, go back and read this chapter again.

GOD'S GUIDE

Read: Ephesians 4:28

- Have you ever cheated on an assignment or test? If you have, what does this verse mean to you? Does God want you to continue to cheat?
- By working hard, you make yourself useful. How does this apply to school? What can you share with classmates if you're caught up on your homework?

_____

_____

_____

_____

BONUS QUESTION

A boy writes a book for all his friends and puts a bonus section at the end of every chapter. If there are 25 chapters, does anyone read it? Please e-mail your answers to: averageboy@family.org

THAT MAKES CENTS!

19

Billy bought a dirt bike! It's black and silver with red stripes. I kept thinking how fast the bike looked as we pushed it to his house. The bike, like all great machines, stopped working right after Billy paid for it.

"Where'd you get the money to buy this?" I asked.

"I planned and saved up," Billy said.

He pulled a notebook out of his backpack and showed me a list of all the money he'd made over the last two years. Here's what it looked like:

Lawns mowed: 43 lawns x $15 a yard = $645

Money for good grades: 0 A's x $10 per A = $0

Cars washed: 22 cars x $5 a car = $110 (minus $12 to buy neighbor a new garden hose = $98)

Coins found under the bleachers at school: $3.28

Lemonade stand: 58 glasses x $1 = $58 (minus $3 for plastic cups and two lemons = $55)

Total profit: $801.28

What's most amazing is that Billy's math was right!

"If you had done this well in math class, you could've earned like 18 more dollars," I said, trying to do the math.

"Well, my sister Giny helped me," he admitted.

"How'd you get her to do that?" I asked.

"I promised her I'd put down the Ping-Pong-ball gun," he said.

Billy is a genius! However, I couldn't help but think that I had mowed more lawns and washed more cars than Billy. And I would've sold more lemonade, except that Billy bought all the lemons at our tiny country store. I knew I'd made more money than he did in the last two years, but I didn't have anything cool to show for it! I wanted a broken-down dirt bike too.

Later that evening, I made a list of all the things I'd bought with the money I'd made:

- 19 CDs (now all scratched or lost)
- 3 bike helmets (one lost in the river and two cracked in half)
- countless candy (all eaten by me—or my dog when I fell asleep on the floor)
- an Atari video-game system (now on the side of the road somewhere in New Mexico)
- 1 trumpet (which my dad has "borrowed" for the last four months)
- 3 Light Sabers (all still in working order, just as soon as I find some duct tape)
- 8 capes (all torn)
- 1 bug collection I bought off Pat (now gone, thanks to the night we played a prank on the girls at camp)
- 4 cans of Silly String (my dad took those after an event we like to call "The Great Shaving Cream Mix-Up")
- 7 cans of Play-Doh (now buried in our living room carpet in an awesome rainbow pattern)
- 1 bag of chipped marbles

What a list! And it didn't even include all the *silly* stuff I had wasted my money on.

Then I checked my "rainy day" money in my piggy bank. Well, I sure hope we have a drought,

because it was empty. That pig had eaten everything! I looked under my bed and found $2.83. I
also checked my pant pockets and located another
50 cents. At least I think it was out of my pockets.
Our dirty laundry basket is so mixed up that it was
hard to tell.

Did You Know?

- Around the world, 8- to 12-year-olds spend an
  estimated $170 billon a year.
- According to a survey done by *kidsmoney.org*,
  the average 10-year-old gets $5 a week in
  allowance.
- Polar bears save their money in *snow banks*.

The point is, I had probably earned more than
a thousand dollars and had only a little over $3 to
show for it.

That's when I decided to start keeping track of
my money. I also decided I wanted to save my
money like Billy. I made a promise to myself not to
spend any money until I'd saved $100.

I started by hiring my brother to keep a money
chart for me. But after two weeks, I realized I was

paying him more than I was making.

"You have to get out there and work harder for us," my brother said as he lay on the couch drinking lemonade.

I couldn't believe it. He hadn't even paid me for that lemonade yet.

I finally figured out that God wants us to properly handle everything He gives us—whether it's talent or money or time. So now I keep track of my money and save it to get something I really want.

Speaking of which, I have to go. I've saved enough money to buy a helmet. I need a new one so I can sit on Billy's superfast broken dirt bike!

Super Average Advice

You've probably heard it said, "Money doesn't grow on trees." But wouldn't it be cool if it did! Everybody would plant an orchard of greenback-producing trees and wait for harvest time. Then it'd be a mad dash to the mall.

Or what if money grew in the ground. You couldn't *beet* that. *Ha!* You could just go outside and rip 24 carrots out of the earth. Get it? Diamonds. Carats. *Help!*

All this money talk can make a person wacky. And that's the problem with money: It *does* make people crazy. Either they go crazy trying to earn it and end up greedy, or they go crazy spending it and end up in debt.

For a lot of kids, a couple of dollars feels like a hot piece of coal—it burns a hole in their pocket. As soon as they get money, they have about 10 ways to spend it. Other kids hoard their cash and won't spend it on anything. As you begin to earn and spend more money, keep these ideas in mind:

Money won't make you happy. A famous story says the richest man in the world was asked how much money would make him happy. His answer: one dollar more. In other words, when your only goal is to make money, you'll never be satisfied. Greed makes you want more. It's not just a problem in our current culture; it was a problem in Jesus' time. Check out what Paul wrote to Timothy: "For the love of money is a root of all kinds of evil, for which some have strayed from the faith in their greediness, and pierced themselves through with many sorrows" (1 Timothy 6:10, NKJV).

When you love money, it changes who you are. Wealth becomes more important than people. And you'll do anything to become rich, whether it means lying, cheating, or stealing.

All money is God's money. God chooses to bless some people with more money than others. If you have a problem with that, take it up with God.

After all, He's God and you're not. We can't always understand His ways, and that's okay.

But some kids like to look around and compare what they have with other families. The problem is, you can always find somebody who has more stuff or better stuff than you, and that can make you feel as though your stuff is inadequate. Comparison can be dangerous. If you want to compare yourself with somebody, think about this fact: More than three billion people in the world live on about $1 per day. If you can watch a TV at home or your family owns a car, you're already one of the richest people on earth.

The Bible says, "And my God will meet all your needs according to his glorious riches in Christ Jesus" (Philippians 4:19). Notice that this verse says "needs," not "wants," and that all your riches can be found in Jesus Christ.

The great thing about God is that even though all money is His, He lets you spend it. All He asks for is 10 percent, or what the Bible calls a tithe. If you want to start managing your money better, try this trick. Use three envelopes. Label one envelope "God," write "future" on another envelope, and put "now" on the last one.

Whenever you get allowance or cash for Christmas or your birthday, divide up your money.

Put at least 10 percent in God's envelope. You may need to ask a parent, grab a calculator, or pay Billy's sister to help you with the math. Then split the rest of your money evenly between the other envelopes, or you may choose to save even more.

Now all you have to do is give God's money to your church, put the "future" money in the bank, and spend the "now" money on whatever you want; for example, you can probably get some chipped marbles for a really good price.

God's Guide

Read: Matthew 6:24-26

- What do you think Jesus meant when He said you can't serve both God and money?
- Why don't you have to worry about money? Who provides for you?
- List some good things you can do with your money.

_____

_____

_____

_____

Put your hand behind your ear with your elbow bent and pointing straight out. Now place a quarter just above your elbow on your forearm. Flip your hand down and try to catch the quarter before it hits the ground. Did you catch it? If so, add 328 more coins. If you catch them all at one time, you just broke the world record!

20

Hi! Billy here, Average Boy's best friend. A.B. asked me to write about living with my dad and stepmom. He wanted me to help him for many reasons:

1. I come from a blended family and he doesn't.

2. His dad took away his computer because we built a really cool fort.

It was awesome. Our fort was made out of a big tarp, some metal poles, and a bunch of old fence boards we found. His dad got mad because we built the fort right behind his car. His dad also said that the old fence boards were still being used as the backyard fence before we found them. A.B. is grounded for a week and asked me to jump in and write about my family.

When my dad married my stepmom, he already had my sister and me. My stepmom also had kids—three, I think. We're all very close.

Hang on. An armadillo just walked into my yard. I'm going to go outside and see if I can catch it.

Okay. I just caught the armadillo and put it in my stepbrother's room. He's going to be so excited because he loves animals!

Anyway, trying to get along is the key to any relationship. That's where the Golden Rule comes in handy. A.B. took me to a church camp once where I learned this: Treat others just as you want to be treated. A.B.'s youth leader said, "You wouldn't want someone going into your room, covering it with toilet paper, and setting off a stink bomb, would you?"

Even though I thought the correct answer was, "Yes, that'd be really cool!" I knew what he meant.

I think that's a really good rule—treat others the same way . . . *Ouch!* Hang on. My stepbrother just came out of his room and threw a flip-flop at me. Evidently he doesn't like *all* kinds of animals. Of course, following the Golden Rule, he must really want to be hit with a flip-flop too. I'll be right back.

Okay. I think it will be easier to write this story in time-out anyway. It's quieter now.

It was really strange when my dad remarried. For a while it was like living with strangers. I didn't know my new stepbrother or stepsisters. All I knew was that they were eating my food and it was harder to watch what I wanted on TV. The first couple of months were difficult because we had to learn new rules.

My stepsisters learned not to walk into my room without knocking, especially if I was having target practice with my Ping-Pong-ball gun. Giny does have a cute dimple now, however!

A.B. told me his story about getting along and doing more stuff with his brother. They're much better friends now. So I tried that. I started treating my stepbrother and stepsisters better. After about a week, they started treating me better too. We still fight some but not as much. Of course, my stepsister and I are about to fight right now because she's making a strange face at me. I'm going to see if I can reach that football on the shelf without getting out of time-out.

Actually, you know what? I reached the football, but I'm not going to throw it. I'm going to do the Golden Rule thing instead. I'm going to smile at her and see what happens.

Man, this Golden Rule thing works. She started laughing. I guess my dad was watching because he just said I could get out of time-out early! Of course, he also said I have to go help my stepbrother catch the armadillo hiding under his bed.

The key thing to remember is that we're a family now with the same responsibilities as any other family. It's not how I expected my family to be, but it's what I've got and I might as well try to make it work. Also, my stepmom loves my dad a lot and makes him happy. That makes me happy, because if Dad is happy, I get in less trouble.

So if you live in a blended family, look for the good points, not the bad. Treat your new brothers and sisters the way you want to be treated—and

Did You Know?

- The United States has one of the highest divorce rates in the world.
- Blended families are a lot more common now than when your parents were growing up.
- Families who drink a lot of juice—so-called "blender" families—will not be discussed in this book.

hide your food and the remote control! Everything will work out.

Anyway, this is Billy signing off. I'd like to thank Average Boy for letting me write this. I'd like to thank you for reading about our adventures in *Focus on the Family Clubhouse* magazine and this book. and I'd also like to thank the armadillo for not doing *that* in my room!

Super Average Advice

Have you gotten into trouble in the last month with someone in your family? It happens, because you're not perfect. Guess what? Adults aren't perfect either. Everybody sins and everyone makes mistakes. Sometimes those mistakes cause relationships to fall apart. Although it's not God's plan, marriages do break up. Chances are, you have a friend who lives in a single-parent home or in a family blended together from other families that have broken apart. Maybe your parents are divorced. While that makes God sad, He also offers people forgiveness and a fresh start.

Of course, it's not easy getting along in a new situation. Maybe your family always put salt on watermelon or ate breakfast cereal with chocolate milk. But now your new family members think that's weird. Do your best to get to know them. Just like a fruit smoothie, blended families can end up being a great combination. If you live in a blended family or with a single parent, there are some things you can remember.

God can turn tough situations into positive ones. Our heavenly Father lets people make their

own choices, even if He might like to force them to do something different. God also allows things to happen that we don't understand: the death of a parent, tornadoes, sickness, the growing of squash.

But that doesn't mean He isn't in control. He always knows what He's doing, even if we can't see His plan. The key is to trust Him. Romans 8:28 (NKJV) says, "And we know that all things work together for good to those who love God." Not everything will make sense to you when it's happening, but you can hang on to the fact that God can turn the hard times in your life into something good. Your attitude will make a big difference. By looking at the positives and trusting God, any situation becomes better.

God will comfort you. God loves you more than anybody in the universe does. When you hurt, He hurts. But He has a limitless supply of peace and comfort to give you. In Psalm 147:3 and 5, the author writes, "He heals the brokenhearted and binds up their wounds. . . . Great is our Lord and mighty in power; his understanding has no limit." God knows when you're sad. He understands your feelings. Talk to Him when life gets hard. No matter what family situation you're in, He'll comfort you.

God's Guide

Read: Colossians 3:12-15
- Does it help you get along with others when you're kind, gentle, and patient?
- According to these verses, what should you do to people who've hurt you?
- Write down some ideas on how love holds people together.

_____

_____

_____

_____

_____

_____

Bonus Tip

Never build a fort behind your dad's car. Build it in your mom's squash garden!

21

My dad took Billy and me to Henry Hippo's Pizza & Prizes. This place has the best pizza in the world if you've never had any other kind of pizza. It's actually so bad that I once ate a big piece before realizing I'd eaten the cardboard box by mistake. I didn't mind though—it was the only time I didn't feel sick afterwards.

We don't go to Henry Hippo's for the pizza. We go for the games! The games cost two tokens each—or $2. My dad says that's a lot of money, but I tell him some of these games last almost a full 20 seconds. Besides, you can't put a price on fun. My dad points out that Henry Hippo has no problem putting a *high* price on fun.

Billy and I try to play games that will hone skills we might need in real life. For instance, I never know when a gopher might poke its head out of the ground at my house. I have to be prepared! Also, if Billy decides to go on the NASCAR tour, he'll be ready.

The games dispense tickets that you can trade for "amazing" prizes—provided that your definition of "amazing" is a pencil with Henry Hippo on it. This particular night, we won 8,000 tickets that we wisely traded for a pencil, some plastic teeth, *and* two mini Tootsie Rolls! How does Henry stay in business when he gives away all that great stuff?

In addition to being excellent at rodent extermination, I also have a real talent for a game called Skee Ball. The object of this game is to get wooden balls into different holes. Each hole gives you a specific number of points. I easily got several balls in a row to drop in the 100,000-points hole, until the manager came over. He told me I had to roll the balls up the ramp toward the holes. He then made me climb off the machine. He started to take away my prize tickets but another employee interrupted us.

"Someone's stuck in the plastic play tunnel!"

he exclaimed.

My dad is always there to save me.

Then Henry Hippo came out to scare the little kids. Parents lined up their crying infants to give the gigantic hippo a hug. I used to be afraid of Henry, too. After all, he's massive. In fact, the last time I talked to him I said, "Henry, you might want to try your salad bar for a change." He just threw some tokens at me, and I won two extra tickets with them!

After we left Henry's, I spent the night at Billy's house. We were supertired, so we decided to watch only three movies. About 1 A.M., I was looking at Billy's stepbrother's DVD collection and found *The Thing That Came from Under the Bed*. It was a horror film. We hesitated. We knew we weren't supposed to watch scary movies.

Billy said, "Let's put it on. We'll probably fall asleep in a few minutes anyway. Besides, how scary can a monster be that comes from under the bed? There's hardly any room under there."

Two hours later Billy and I were huddled together under a blanket. We weren't breathing. We didn't want any monsters to know where we were. Billy's eyes were actually bigger than his head and my hair was sticking straight up. I could feel each individual hair.

"T-t-t-turn it off," I said.

"You turn it off," Billy said. "The remote is over on that spooky chair."

"It's your TV," I argued.

"You're the superhero," Billy said.

Man, sometimes it's no fun being a superhero. I crawled out from under the blanket and inched my way toward the chair. I kept looking around for The Thing That Came from Under the Bed just in case it decided to change its name to The Thing That Jumped on the Living Room Chair! I reached the chair and stretched out one shaky hand to hit the Off button. Huge mistake! Now the room was completely dark. One thing we'd learned from the movie was that The Thing That Came from Under the Bed could see in the dark! I desperately tried to find the remote.

Suddenly, I heard an evil voice: "UUH-HAAAAHHHAAAA!" I froze.

Billy and I didn't have time to think. We could only react. We jumped into action and hit The Yawning Thing That Came Down the Stairs with our only weapons: a Henry Hippo pencil and some plastic teeth. The voice started yelling again, and an arm reached for the light switch. It was Billy's dad yawning as he came downstairs to check on us.

That night we learned why our parents don't

want us watching certain movies. Billy's dad explained that if we watch bad movies, those images get burned in our brains. Entertainment choices affect our minds forever. I thought Billy's dad made some good points, even though it was hard to take him seriously with those plastic teeth in his mouth.

Super Average Advice

If you lived about 100 years ago, your entertainment options would've consisted of a wooden hoop, a stick, a homemade doll (really a stick with a rag over it), and a rock. Pretty hard to get in trouble with those—unless there were any really big windows nearby. Today you have more kinds of entertainment than entrées at an all-you-can-eat Chinese buffet. A lot has happened in 100 years.

Radios became popular during the 1920s. That's the same time that silent movies were the rage. Sound hit the theaters in the 1930s. In the late '30s, tiny black-and-white TVs came on the market. But television didn't become really huge until the 1960s. Video-game consoles and CDs all rode the wave of technology in the last 30 years.

A hundred years ago, you'd have had a hard time finding entertainment with any objectionable content. Now you can turn on the TV and find people wearing next to nothing (or less if you have cable), cussing, and shooting at each other. Thousands of years ago Solomon wrote some words that are more true today than they've ever been: "Above all else, guard your heart, for it is the well-spring of life" (Proverbs 4:23).

Every day you must make the decision to guard your heart. A lot of kids aren't doing a very good job. Forty percent of fifth-graders say they've seen an R-rated movie. If you're not careful, the media will fill your mind with junk. Try this plan to

Did You Know?

- In a survey of 11- to 16-year-olds who play video games, 25 percent said an M-rated game was their favorite. In some states, M-rated games can be sold only to people 17 and over.
- In 1965, NBC became the first full-color network and some of their shows were only in black and white.
- The game Kick the Can was outlawed in the 1930s because it was too violent.*

* Not really, but you have to feel sorry for the can.

keep that from happening:

Listen to your Spirit. God gave everybody a conscience that helps us know right from wrong. As a Christian, you have something way better! The Holy Spirit lives inside you to help guide your decisions. You know when you're seeing something you shouldn't. At those times, you must choose to get away from the situation. That's not always easy because kids may make fun of you. Plus, everyone has a sinful nature that nudges him to go against God's will. Galatians 5:16 says, "So I say, live by the Holy Spirit's power. Then you will not do what your sinful nature wants you to do" (NIrv). God's Spirit will help you do the right thing and make the best choices. But you have to choose to listen to Him.

Use your head. All entertainment contains a message. Every TV show you watch, every song you listen to, every movie you see, every video game you play teaches you something. You may learn how violent some people can be. You may get the message that it's okay to be selfish and rude to other people.

Engage your brain when you're consuming entertainment. Think about what it's trying to teach you, weigh that message against God's standards, and follow Paul's advice in Colossians 2:8: "See to it that no one takes you captive through hollow and deceptive philosophy, which depends on human tradition and the basic principles of this world rather than on Christ."

It's easy to start believing "deceptive philosophies" from the world. Keep your guard up and look to Jesus as your example. Whenever you watch a movie or play a video game, ask yourself, "Would I be comfortable doing this if Jesus was sitting right beside me?" The answer to that question will be a great guide as you make your way through the entertainment buffet.

BONUS ACTIVITY

Nothing good on TV? If you or your friends have a video camera, you can make your own movie. Billy and I have done this. We started by acting out scenes in the Bible. It was fun until Billy (who was playing Goliath) read the end of the scene and ran away screaming!

GOD'S GUIDE

Read: Philippians 4:8-9

- Do your entertainment choices live up to being true, pure, and holy?
- Why do you think God stresses the importance of protecting your mind?
- If you've made poor choices with entertainment in the past, write a prayer to God asking for forgiveness and decide now to be wiser in the future.

_____

_____

_____

_____

_____

_____

_____

22

"Donny has really bad breath," I said to my friend Pat. "I bet he could breathe on a match and it would light itself in self-defense!"

Pat seemed preoccupied watching other people eat in the lunchroom. He didn't smile. Didn't laugh. Nothing.

However, an hour later Donny walked up to me after eating what must've been a tuna and onion sandwich. "I heard you said I have bad health," he said. "You think I'm so weak I couldn't even blow out a match or defend myself!"

I couldn't believe it spread that quickly—the

rumor, not Donny's breath. And like most gossip, it got switched and changed around until it didn't sound like what was said in the first place.

"I said you had bad *breath*!" I pleaded, realizing too late that this wouldn't get me off the hook.

Gossip is a horrible thing. My school is full of it. In fact, you know who gossips the most? Wait, if I tell you, then I'll be gossiping.

Sometimes it's hard to know what's gossip and what's information that needs to be shared. For example, if a shark is attacking someone, I'm pretty sure you should tell a lifeguard about it. But if someone has something bad or embarrassing happen, you probably shouldn't spread it around.

Last year, a lot of kids at school started gossiping that I liked this girl named Jennifer. I told only one person, which might have been fine if the microphone hadn't been on.

You see, my principal lets me make the morning announcements on the intercom every day. One morning I said, "Hey, everyone! Average Boy here to let you know about the school talent show. All you talented people, sign up. The rest of you without talent—and we know who you are thanks to last year's talent show—can come out, too, because we need audience members. On a personal note, we're encouraging students not to boo this year. Which reminds me: My band, 'Big Bob B and the Alliterations,' will be performing again. And if anyone is listening in room 123 right now, please explain to Donny what *alliteration* means."

That's when my principal interrupted me.

"Bob! Didn't we decide you should read the announcements exactly as they're written?"

"Okay," I joked. "But I'll need a pen to write down my changes."

Next, I had to play a few prerecorded messages. I put in the tape and hit Play. At least I thought I hit Play. Turns out I pushed Pause, so the entire school could hear what my principal said next.

"So are you excited about the talent show?" she asked.

"Yeah," I answered. "I might invite this girl named Jennifer so she can see me play my triangle! Speaking of, can you pass a rule that stops kids from throwing things while the talent is performing?"

"Bob, I can't control an angry mob," my principal said.

That's when the school secretary stepped into the room.

"The microphone is still on," she said.

"Oh no!" I said.

"By the way," our secretary continued, "which

Jennifer? There are six, you know."

Even our school secretary was caught up in the gossip! I grabbed the microphone and tried to recover.

"And we're back. Some of you may have just heard the principal and me practicing a skit for the talent show called, 'Who Likes Jennifer?' It's going to be great!"

No one fell for it. For the next week, everyone tried to guess which Jennifer I liked. Three of the

Did You Know?

- The little red bumps on your tongue are called taste buds because they're friends and spread rumors about which foods they like best.*
- Sixty-five percent of what people talk about could be called gossip.
- Some middle schoolers spread mean rumors about others to become more popular. But studies show these same people lose popularity in high school because others grow tired of them being cruel.

* Come on, you know taste buds can't talk! They use smoke signals to communicate.

Jennifers even came up and told me that they were busy the night of the talent show.

"You aren't the Jennifer!" I said.

"Just making sure," they said.

The funny thing is, I didn't like any of the Jennifers at my school. The Jennifer I liked went to my church! However, gossip doesn't care if it's right or wrong.

I finally got the gossip to stop on the night of the talent show. Standing on stage, I said, "This song goes out to all six Jennifers. It's called 'I Promise You Aren't the One.' I hope you like it. Hey, can you wait to throw things until after we start playing?"

The point is, I should've known not to say anything about Donny. It's always best to think about what you're saying at all times. If what you're about to say might hurt someone's feeling, don't say it.

Now if you'll excuse me, I have to go apologize to Donny—just as soon as I find him some breath mints.

Super Average Advice

Words hurt. Don't believe it? Lift a dictionary over your head and drop it on your foot. *Ouch!* See, words do hurt.

The person who said, "Sticks and stones can

break my bones, but words can never hurt me," was probably never called "loser" or "stupid," or had mean rumors about him spread everywhere. Comments like that *are* painful. They leave scars.

One of the most dangerous things about words is that they can't be ripped out of thin air and placed back in your mouth. Once a word escapes your lips, it's out there. You can try to take back what you say and ask for forgiveness, but many times the damage is already done. That's why it's always a good idea to think carefully before you speak. Here are a couple of reasons why:

The tongue is powerful. Not only is the tongue one of the strongest muscles in your body (try lying flat on your face and doing a tongue push-up), but it also forms every word that leaves your mouth. Don't let that little red muscle fool you into thinking its only purpose is to taste food and lick ice-cream cones. Jesus' younger brother James wrote, "The tongue is the most evil part of the body. It pollutes the whole person" (James 3:6, NIrV).

Those are strong words. They probably hurt the tongue's feelings. Poor tongue.

But James also says the sign of a mature person is the ability to control the tongue (James 3:2). You can tell a lot about a person by the things that come out of his mouth.

Think about what you might say in these situations:

• You smash your thumb with a hammer while trying to build a fence.

• You hear your class's straight-A student flunked a test because she forgot to study.

• A group of kids is making fun of a new student and invites you to join in.

Would your tongue form kind and good words in these scenarios? Would filthy and hurtful language fly out of your mouth? Or would you be asking yourself, *Why am I building a fence?*

Gossip hurts relationships. If you're known for spreading rumors or cutting people down, chances are you'll be pretty lonely. Proverbs 11:13 says, "A gossip betrays a confidence, but a trustworthy man keeps a secret."

When you spread a secret, you lose trust. When you make up a nasty rumor, you damage another person. People want friends they can count on—not friends that run on at the mouth. By watching your words, you'll get yourself in less trouble and become somebody that others want to be around.

God's Guide

Read: Romans 1:28-31

- Look at the list of wicked things people do when they don't follow God. Does anything on the list surprise you?
- Why do you think gossiping is included in this list?
- Explain why you think gossiping is so dangerous.

_____

_____

_____

_____

Bonus Activity

Organize a bad-breath competition. Invite your friends to eat anything in your house for 30 seconds. Then vote to see who has the worst breath. The winner gets to deeply exhale on each person one more time! (Note: This game is best played right when you wake up after eating onion pizza the night before!)

23

This has to be my biggest adventure yet. I have a girlfriend!

I'd better start a new paragraph, because you probably need some time to let it sink in. Actually, she's not my girlfriend. I'm not even allowed to date. But I can invite a girl to school functions, and that's what I did! Oh, my dad said I should point out that it wasn't my mom or anyone else in my family.

I've always had trouble with girls. The first time I tried to ask a girl to a school function, it didn't go well. I was drinking a Slurpee and got a

Growing Up Super Average

brain freeze in the middle of asking her.

"Hi, I'm Bob," I said.

Then the brain freeze hit. My face wrinkled up and I started hitting my face just above my right eye. "Would you like to—Ooooooooooouch *(slap, slap)* Ugggg *(Slap, slap)* My Eye Ooohhhh *(slap, slap)* Ohhhhh, butter pecan pancakes! *(slap, slap!)* Auggghhhh!"

I don't know what came over me. I actually prefer apple cinnamon pancakes. When my massive head pain went away, I smiled and said, "So will you go to the school ice cream social with me?"

Anyway, the girl just stared at me and then turned and walked away. Evidently, she didn't like pancakes.

Another time I had trouble when our youth leader wanted us to hold hands for the closing prayer. I quickly looked to my right. No one was there. However, when I looked to my left, I saw Christy. She held out her hand. That's when I realized we will never have a drought in my town. If it ever doesn't rain for a month, I will simply hold Christy's hand and produce enough water to flood the entire city. My hand actually started dripping as she reached for it!

During the prayer (which lasted about seven hours), her hand slipped out of mine several times.

However, she just wiped off her hand and grabbed mine again. When the prayer finally ended, I looked up.

"Man, the humidity in this room is ridiculous!" I said, trying to hide my nervousness.

Anyway, back to my girlfriend—I mean, the girl who agreed to go with me to a school function. Last week I walked up to Wendy and said, "Would you like to go with me to the athletic banquet?"

She actually nodded her head up and down!

"Great," I said.

Then I tapped her on the shoulder and said my parents and I would pick her up at 6 P.M.

"What?" Wendy asked, taking off her headphones. She listens to really loud music. I've heard that listening to loud music is bad for your hearing. Now I know it really messes up your short-term memory, too. She didn't even remember what I'd just asked her.

I explained that we were going to the athletic banquet together. I reminded her how she had nodded so intently when I invited her.

She laughed really hard and told me to pick her up at 6 o'clock! Wendy is really nice. In fact, that's why I asked her. I know that Jesus wants me to hang out only with girls who love Him.

There were some problems however. When I

picked her up, I suddenly lost the ability to speak. I wanted to say, "Hi, you look nice." But what came out was, "Nice, you look hi!"

She laughed again and said, "I'll put on some shoes with smaller heels."

When we got in my parents' car, love was in the air! There was so much kissing going on that I finally said, "Uh, Mom and Dad? Can you stop that and drive us to the banquet?" It was embarrassing, but Wendy was laughing.

Did You Know?

- God created marriage to be between one man and one woman.
- Studies find that the average age people develop their first "crush" is 10.
- Billy told Donny, who told Austin, who told Mark, who told Mary that Bob thinks Wendy is cute.

When we arrived at school, I was so nervous that I forgot to open her door. I forgot to open my door as well. Wendy eventually jumped out and opened my door for me. Before we walked in, I knew I had to say something: "I probably won't get an award tonight, like the players do, but I do hold the school record for most water bottles run out onto the football field."

"I don't care," she said. "I just like that you're always yourself. It's a little strange sometimes, but it's always interesting. Let's just have fun!"

That's when I learned if you're always yourself, you don't have to be nervous around the opposite sex.

Now if you will excuse me, I have to tell my parents to stop kissing because Wendy has to be home by 9:30.

Super Average Advice

When God created everything, He had a perfect plan. He carefully designed every living thing. He formed everything with a purpose. It's no accident that girls like boys and that boys are attracted to girls. God made it that way! It's natural. God even said, "It is not good for the man to be alone. I will make a helper who is just right for him" (Genesis 2:18, NIrV). Then God created the first woman.

As you grow up, your opinion of the opposite sex will change from when you were younger. Instead of thinking they have "cooties," you'll discover there are a lot of "cuties." And that's good.

What you do with these feelings and emotions is important. Every family has different rules about dating, but there are some standards you should always remember.

Treat the opposite sex with respect. Not only is your body the temple of the Holy Spirit (1 Corinthians 6:19), so is every other believer's. Because God lives in you, you need to protect and honor your body.

But what does it look like to respect the opposite sex? Good question. (I know, I wrote it!)

It means you don't use crude language to describe them. It means you don't try to make them do things they don't want to do. It means you look at their inward beauty, instead of outward appearance. It means you talk with them like fellow children of Christ. Of course, maybe your conversations sound something like this.

Patrick: That math homework was totally hard.
Jennifer: (*Giggle. Giggle.*)
Patrick: It took me like an hour to finish it.
Jennifer: Yeah. (*Giggle.*) Me too.
Patrick: Who do you like better: Batman or Superman?
Jennifer: Wonder Woman.
Patrick: Uh . . . yeah. Me too.
Talking with the opposite sex does become

easier. As you get older, it'll become more natural to be yourself, and to share your thoughts and feelings. The best relationships are built through talking and understanding. It just takes time. Speaking of which . . .

Take your time. Society puts a lot of pressure on you to grow up quickly. Kids on TV shows and movies wear makeup, flirt with the opposite sex, and go on dates. The Bible paints a different picture.

If you read the story of Jacob in Genesis 29, you'll see that he worked and waited seven years to marry Rachel. Then he worked another seven years on Rachel's dad's farm before he left. Jacob didn't rush. He took his time getting to know Rachel before they married. His love for her grew. He showed a lot of patience.

But many people lack patience today. They get frustrated waiting for the microwave to heat up a pizza roll.

Remember that you have a lot of time before you get married. You'll meet a lot of people. Most don't meet their future spouse until their college years or beyond. For now, it's best to be patient and decide what qualities you want for a future husband or wife. Do you want to marry somebody who's cute, funny, smart, hardworking, athletic, musical, strong, friendly, talkative, creative, nice, thoughtful? Above all, decide to look for somebody who loves God and wants to serve Him.

And if you feel as though nobody likes you right now, that's okay. Be patient. God has a plan. Trust Him with your future, and focus on becoming the person He wants you to be. God has designed your future, and it's better than you can imagine.

GOD'S GUIDE

Read: Ephesians 5:28-33

- Reading about marriage may seem weird, but there are some important ideas in these verses. How should a husband treat his wife? How should a wife treat her husband?
- Write down a few ideas from these verses that you can use in future relationships with the opposite sex.

_____

_____

_____

_____

If you get tongue-tied around the opposite sex, learn a new language like Pashto or Urdu. People with a foreign accent are always popular.

24

My dad has a hard time getting a good radio signal in our van. I feel kind of bad about it. But in my defense, the van's antenna did make a perfect sword the day Billy and I took up fencing. Now when we drive, we get only a few local radio channels that are owned by farmers that broadcast just when they aren't plowing.

Our favorite is WAKO radio, a small station actually run on two AA batteries. Ted is the farmer/DJ. We like his station because of the contests.

Between songs, he also keeps his listeners up to date on the latest news: "That song was 'How Can I

Miss You If You Don't Leave?' Now for the news. My ingrown toenail feels much better. My boys caught a rabbit last night. The store got a few more lemons in yesterday. This has been Ted's News—fair and balanced. Now back to the music."

One day as my family drove to town, my dad reached over and hit the scan button on the radio. The numbers flew past until the scanner landed on 88.7, which turned out to be the instrumental music channel. This station played music that was too boring even for elevators. The songs included "Sounds of Air" and "Sounds of Air Not Good Enough to Make It on the First Song." Every so often the DJ came on to wake people up. One time he asked for requests. I called and asked if he had any earplugs.

Anyway, "Rivers of Nebraska" was playing. I waited for my dad to change the station . . . and I waited.

"Dad, are you asleep?" I asked. "If you can hear me, please change the station!"

My dad looked at me through the rearview mirror and smiled. "I think we'll listen to this while we think back to why we don't have an antenna."

Uuuugggggg! It was horrible. I could feel my body going numb as boredom seeped into my brain. I reached into my pockets to see if I had anything to plug my ears. I'm glad I did, because I found a frog that should have been taken out two hours ago. I also discovered three cracked marbles, some unused Henry Hippo's tickets, and a rubber, sticky hand attached to a stretchy cord. The cord could stretch about three feet, which gave me an idea.

My plan was to sling the hand between Dad and Mom and hit one of the radio buttons to change the channel. I prayed about it. (I've learned to always pray before trying one of my plans.) I threw the sticky hand at the radio. Not only did it hit a button, but it flipped the radio to a loud rock station. The radio quickly went from the soothing "Rivers of Nebraska" to the deafening sound of "Kaboom! Do you hear the explosion? Here it is again—Kaboom!"

"Auuuuuggggggghhhhhhhhhh!!!!!!!!!~!!!" my dad screamed. (How he screamed "~" I'll never know.)

The music scared him so badly that he started swerving all over the road. My marbles and Henry Hippo tickets went flying. I was thrown back into my seat and then thrust forward. The problem was that I still held the stretchy cord. The sticky hand ripped away from the radio and headed toward me. Right as it got between my mom and dad, he quickly swerved right. The sticky hand curved around and stuck to my dad's face.

I thought Dad knew I had one of those hand things. Evidently not. He totally freaked out when the gooey hand grabbed his face.

"Auuuuuu~uhhhhhh~hhh!!!~!!" Dad screamed again. (Man, he was generous with the "~"s that time!)

Did You Know?

- The first set of Roman laws—called the Twelve Tables—was published 450 years before Jesus' birth. Every Roman who went to school had to memorize them.
- In Alabama, it's illegal for a driver to be blind-folded while operating a vehicle.
- A real law in Nebraska states that a parent may be arrested if his child can't hold back a burp during a church service.

Note: Actually, all three of these are true.

He grabbed the rubber hand and threw it out the window. I scared Dad even more by shouting, "My hand! That's my hand!"

With the hand gone, I figured everything would be fine. However, my brother turned around and said, "That's so cool. The hand landed on that police officer's windshield!"

Twenty minutes later we finished telling the story to the officer. He laughed so hard, he could barely write out a ticket. It was a great lesson on respecting authority.

One of my dad's rules is to never throw things in the van. I thought he just didn't want to be bothered. I never thought it was a danger issue. Adults have a lot of silly rules—or at least they may seem silly. However, God wants us to respect and obey people in authority because they put rules in place to protect us, even if we don't understand.

So I hope you learn from my mistake—a mistake I'm still paying for. That ticket was superexpensive!

Anyway, we finally pulled back on the road and everything settled down—until my frog hopped on Mom's leg.

Super Average Advice

As a kid, it can feel like everyone bosses you around. Teachers give you homework. Parents ask you to get off your brother. Police officers make sure you don't ride your skateboard on the sidewalk. Your dog demands that you feed it. It seems as if everybody has power—but you.

At times when you feel like you're being dumped on, just remember that you can always order the cat to stop scratching your leg. (It won't listen, but you *can* yell at it.) Instead of becoming frustrated by the authorities in your life, God gives you a different plan.

Show honor. *Honor* is a weird word that most people don't use anymore, unless they're trying to describe a really good school band or a difficult class. But this word appears in more than 160 verses of the *New International Version* Bible. In almost every occasion, it means to display proper respect.

First Peter 2:17 puts it this way: "Show proper respect to everyone: Love the brotherhood of believers, fear God, honor the king." This verse not only tells us to respect authorities, but to show "proper" respect to everybody, including fellow Christians, God, and government officials.

Submit to authority. Honoring authorities is a decision that will show in your attitude. Submission to authority shows in your actions. Sometimes you won't understand the rules, such as:

- Don't run with scissors.
- Don't play in traffic.
- Don't hit somebody when you're angry.
- Don't destroy other people's property.

Okay, those aren't good examples because I

know you understand them. But even if you don't fully understand a rule, it's still important for you to obey it. Hebrews 13:17 says, "Obey your leaders. Put yourselves under their authority. They keep watch over you. They know they are accountable to God for everything they do. Obey them so that their work will be a joy. If you make their work a heavy load, it won't do you any good" (NIrV).

Obviously, you care about the decisions that the authorities in your life make, including parents, teachers, principals, and law enforcement officers. But God cares even more and will judge them based on their actions. Being in a position of authority is a tough job. Do your best not to add any stress and to make things more enjoyable for your authorities.

BONUS ACTIVITY

Rubber sticky hands are great for picking up paper lying on the floor or waking your brother up for church. You can get them for a dollar at a store or nine dollars at Henry Hippo's Pizza & Prizes.

Read: Romans 13:1-5

- How do you feel knowing that only God can give authority to rulers? Does it make you want to follow them more?
- Who needs to be afraid of the authorities?
- Who is ultimately responsible for punishing wrongdoers?

_____

_____

_____

_____

_____

_____

_____

ULTIMATE DIRT REMOVAL SYSTEM

25

I had never written a book before this. I've colored a few but never written one. I hope you liked it. If not, there are some blank pages in here you can draw on. And if you didn't write on the lines in God's Guide at the end of each chapter, your mom can use them for grocery lists. So either way, my book was worth the money you spent—unless, of course, you stole this book. Then you need to go back and reread the sections on stealing!

I've got just one more adventure I want to tell you about. But remember, you can read my stories every month in *Focus on the Family Clubhouse* magazine! (Look at the end of this book for details or log on to www.averageboy.org.)

Anyway, last week it rained really hard. I didn't want to open the front door, because the hallway carpet would get wet. I explained this to my brother, but he didn't believe me. He just kept banging on the door and shouting, "Let me in! Let me in!"

Finally, it stopped raining, and I opened the door and joined my soaking-wet brother outside. The ditch in front of our house had turned into a three-foot-deep river. When this happens, we usually swing from a tree rope into the water. It's a lot of fun, and we get really muddy. I couldn't wait! I climbed the tree, grabbed the rope, and launched into the air!

SPLOOOOOSSSHHHHH!

"*Ha, ha!* You missed me!" I yelled, still holding on to the rope. (My brother sometimes throws things at me while I'm swinging.) I then did a triple-gainer into the water!

For the next 20 minutes, my brother and I pretended to be twin Tarzans. We swam. We swung. We dove. We wrestled and captured a very, very angry alligator.

Then I tried for the ultimate jump and swung out a little farther before I let go of the rope. I went crashing into the water and instantly felt a sharp pain in my hip. At first I thought it was my dog seeking revenge for making him pretend to be an alligator. Then I looked up and saw our "alligator" tied up and still very, very angry!

I reached under the water and felt a large rock. I didn't think much about it, because I normally don't swing that far into the ditch. I started walking upstream, but for some reason I felt like I should look at that rock again, so I walked over, grabbed it, and hauled it up.

Well, it wasn't a rock at all. It was a turtle! And not just any kind of turtle; it was a land turtle. Land turtles can't swim because of their short arms. I'm sure it's impossible for them to keep their floaties on. The turtle was drowning, and God used me to save it!

Just as Jesus saved me from eternal death, God used me to save the turtle from dying. I felt so good, until my brother said, "We can take him to the basketball game."

That's when I remembered my dad's words to me: "You can go outside but don't get muddy. We have a basketball game to go to in an hour."

I looked down at my skin and clothes. Not good. I actually looked like Willy Wonka had made me out of chocolate.

"Brian, we aren't supposed to get muddy," I said. "Dad's going to be furious!"

"Maybe we can offer him a peace turtle," my brother said.

I knew we were in supertrouble. That's when I felt a big, fat drop of rain hit my head. I grinned. God is so good. Huge raindrops started showering down on my brother and me. Two minutes later we were as clean as if we'd just taken a shower, which we kind of had.

It just reminded me how Jesus washes away all the bad stuff in our lives. Jesus cleans away our sins. He leaves us fresh and new. If you are drowning in the dirty things you do and want to be made clean, you can turn to Jesus. He'll lift you up and save you forever.

Did You Know?

- Sixty-four percent of young people believe that a person will go to heaven if he or she acts nicely toward others and does good things.
- The word *Christian* means "follower of Christ."
- Eternity is way longer than it takes to heat up a pizza roll, so it's a good idea to know where you'll spend yours.
  Note: Sorry, no jokes this time.

Super Average Advice

Choosing to believe in Jesus Christ is the most important decision you'll ever make. Sure, you have other important choices in your life:

- what clothes you'll wear tomorrow;
- whether you'll try out for basketball or band;
- what friends you'll hang out with;
- what career you'll want when you grow up;
- who you'll marry;
- whether to gel or not to gel your hair. (That's a big one!)

Those are all important decisions. Some choices will influence your sense of style. Some will affect the quality of your day. And others will determine the success of your life.

But the decision to follow Jesus will affect your *forever*. It will determine where you spend eternity. Will you choose to believe in God and live with Him forever when you die? Or will you turn your back on God, follow your own wishes, and live forever away from Him?

The choice is up to you. God doesn't make anybody believe in Him. He gave every human being free will—or the ability to make his or her own choice. He created us to worship Him, but He wants us to do it willingly. If you haven't made the decision to follow Jesus, think about these things:

Forgiveness is a gift. Nobody can *earn* forgiveness, yet everybody needs it. Everyone has disobeyed God's rules, whether it's lying to parents, thinking bad thoughts about somebody, treating a brother poorly, or cheating at school. The Bible calls that disobedience sin.

God is a perfectly holy God, who demands total righteousness for anybody who enters heaven. We could never live up to God's standards, so He gives us a gift to save us. Ephesians 2:8-9 (NIrv) says, "God's grace has saved you because of your faith in Christ. Your salvation doesn't come from anything you do. It is God's gift. It is not based on anything you have done. No one can brag about earning it."

When you put your faith in Jesus Christ, He forgives your sins. He wipes out all the dirty stuff you've done and makes you perfectly clean and holy in God's eyes.

Jesus is the only way to heaven. Some people believe that if they do enough good things, God will have to let them into heaven. But that's not what the Bible says. Look at these two verses:

• "For God so loved the world that he gave his one and only Son, that whoever believes in him shall not perish but have eternal life" (John 3:16).

• "Jesus said to him, 'I am the way, the truth,

and the life. No one comes to the Father except through Me' " (John 14:6, NKJV).

God doesn't want people to be separated from Him. He wants everybody to be saved, so He made it possible for everybody to come to heaven by sending Jesus to earth to die for our sins. When Jesus said, "No one comes to the Father except through Me," He meant exactly that—He's the *only* way. All we have to do is believe.

Going to church won't make you a Christian any more than hanging out in the kitchen will make you a great chef. You have to make a decision and pray to follow Jesus.

If you want to choose to follow Jesus now, you can pray this prayer (or something like it) and know without a doubt that you'll spend forever with God:

Dear God, please forgive me. I know I am a sinner. I believe Jesus Christ died, came back to life, and rose to heaven so I could be forgiven of my sins and live forever with You. I accept Your gift of forgiveness. Thank You for rescuing me. From this day, I'll do everything I can to follow You. Amen.

If you just prayed, congratulations! Welcome to God's family. Now go tell a friend, your youth pastor, or your parents about your new life in Christ. And e-mail me at **averageboy@family.org** so I can celebrate with you.

GOD'S GUIDE

Read: Romans 3:22-24
- According to these verses, who has sinned or made mistakes that go against God's law?
- Is it possible for somebody to do enough good things to erase the bad?
- Who makes you righteous in God's eyes?

_____

_____

_____

_____

_____

BONUS FACT

Turtles may bite you—whether you save them or not! Oh, and you should ask your parents' permission before swimming in any ditch. The ditch in front of our house is harmless, but kids have actually drowned in drainage ditches. Always ask first.

Average Boy Online

Visit Average Boy online at **www.averageboy.org**. You can play games, solve puzzles, e-mail Average Boy, and look at some of his past helpful e-mails. Here's a sample:

Yo, Average Boy!

Have you ever tried to memorize something, and it feels like it doesn't want to stay in your brain? Do you have any suggestions for memorization?
Rachel

Hey, Rachel!

Yes. I'm very good at . . . uh . . . what were

we talking about? Oh, yeah, memorizing! First of all, you have to work out your mind just like your body. I've been exercising my brain for years, and now it's as strong as a steel . . . uh . . . something. What's that phrase again? Well, it's strong.

Also, Julie, you really have to pay attention to details so your mind holds on to the information. Concentrate really hard on what you want to mem-orize and . . . *ha, ha* . . . this commercial with a duck just came on, and it was hilarious!

Anyway, Eddie, I hope that answers your question.

Your friend and mine,

Average Boy

Dear Average Boy,

I am 11 years old, four-foot-three-inches tall, and the shortest kid in my fifth-grade class. What should I do when people start teasing me?

Signed,

Short Stuff

Hey, Short Stuff!

I think you should get a ladder, look your teaser right in the eye, and say, "Look, Jolly Green Giant! I like being short. When it rains, I'm the last to get wet. Plus, I'll always have a job at the Chocolate

Factory! Not to mention, I'll win limbo contests for the rest of my grade school career. When you want to go mountain climbing, you have to go to Colorado, but all I have to do is find a speed bump. Short is cool!"

That's what I'd say. Actually, that is what I do say because I'm not on the tall side either. I just laugh it off because I know God made me the way I am for a reason. I don't let other kids make me feel bad about it. You sound as though you have a good sense of humor about it as well. Keep it up and keep reading!

Your short friend and mine,

Average Boy

Dear AB,

I think your stories are very funny. Do you have any nicknames? I do. My older sister gave me the nickname "Nikkik." In Ojibwe, a language the natives here speak, it means "otter." She gave me that name because in the winter I would slide down a hill of snow without a sled. Have you ever done that?

Nikkik

Hey, Otter!

I used to slide down hills all the time, but then I quit walking so close to my dad when we were near a drop-off. As for a nickname, all my friends at school have given me tons of them. Here are a few examples:

1. Hey, you!
2. Kid
3. Yo
4. Bob (which in English—a language the natives speak here—means "Cool Guy")

There are many more, but you get the idea how popular I am. Thanks for reading my stories, and I'd like to say something in Ojibwe: *Nikkik.* (That's the only word I know in Ojibwe.) Have fun sliding down those hills!

Your friend and mine,

Average Boy

More Great Resources
from Focus on the Family®

Adventures in Odyssey Novels
by Paul McCusker

Mark Prescott is the new kid in Odyssey—and he doesn't want to be there. His parents have split up, and the only one who wants to be his friend is an annoying girl. But not all's bad. At an ice cream shop called Whit's End, there's a quirky inventor named John Whittaker who seems to create fun and adventure for the whole town. As Mark gets drawn into life in Odyssey, what he learns will change his life. Paperback.

Passages Fantasy Fiction Series
by Paul McCusker

Written in the style of C.S. Lewis's *Narnia* series, *Passages* books begin in small-town Odyssey and take you to an extraordinary land where two moons light the night sky, visitors discover strange powers, and belief in God becomes the adventure of a lifetime! Each of the six novels includes a collectible map of Marus. Paperback.

Dare 2 Share: A Field Guide to Sharing Your Faith
by Greg Stier

Now that you've learned about developing your relationship with God, you've got something exciting to share! Greg Stier will help equip you with new boldness to express your faith to anyone, anywhere through this awesome witnessing plan. Learn how to talk and listen to friends who are atheists, Buddhists, and more. Paperback.